PRAISE FOR
NIRVANA

"[*Nirvana* is an] intriguing meld of virtual reality, species extinction, and corporate evil."

—Wendy Stephens, Director, *United States Board on Books for Young People*

"If you enjoy futuristic what-if books like *The Hunger Games* or *The Matrix,* give this series a read."

—Victoria Harvey, *Ivy's Ecclectic Reviews*

"I believe this is less a doomsday premise than it is a wake up call."

—Barb Heck, *Goodreads*

"This is the absolutely best work of fiction about virtual reality that I have ever read. The blurring of the line between reality and virtual reality has never been more powerfully displayed in anything I have read."

—Rhetta Akamatsu, *Blog Critics Magazine*

"J.R. Stewart has written a masterpiece. Combining a post-apocalyptic dystopian society with virtual reality is sheer genius . . . this is a dystopian society book that you simply must read."

—Charli Gamble, *The Goth Girl Reads*

"This book had my attention from the very beginning. The further into the book I got, the more nervous I became. Well written, and a little nerve wracking given how close to reality it is."

—Debbie Young, *Goodreads*

"This is so much more than just a story set in the future, this could literally be our reality. This book has left me with a nagging feeling that one day someone looking back in history will say, 'Didn't someone once write about this happening in a book?'"

—Susan Hampson, *Goodreads*

"I want my own kids to read this for the lessons in the story. Virtual reality and the lure of mental escape is not a substitute for paying attention to politics."

—Cat Jennings, book reviewer

"So many questions in this wonderful beginning! Take a chance to enjoy a great read."

—Laurie Monical, educator

"This book is filled with surprises, making it impossible to put down."

—Sandra Brazier, *Goodreads*

"The whole book flows nicely, and you are left wanting the rest of the series to hurry up and come out so you can continue on with finding out the truths."

—Karen Teague, *Critique Corner*

"The ending left me hanging, then I realized it was one of three! Bring on the other two. I need to know what happens next."

—Douglas Osler, book reviewer

"Stewart creates a new world with this novel. A world that has worlds within it. As well as plots, different schemes, friendship, skewed friendship, hate, treachery, back-stabbing, etc. This book has so many things in it but it works."

—Denise Wheelock, *Goodreads*

"In this book, J.R. Stewart cleverly disguises his concern about virtual reality and the powers over the public that it gives to its creator. Through his book, he really makes the reader reconsider the truth in his or her daily life."

—Sandra Brazier, *Goodreads*

"The cover of this book drew me in right away, and after reading the synopsis, I definitely knew it would be something I would like, and I was right."

—Sheila Roposa, *Goodreads*

"This is my first book by J.R. Stewart and it won't be my last."

—Simera King, *Goodreads*

"*Nirvana* by J. R. Stewart, an amazing story by a very skillful writer, started out interestingly enough, where a secret was formed in the darkness that caused a situation to come up in which there could be no escape."

—Wanda Maynard, advance reviewer

COPYRIGHT INFORMATION

Nirvana (Nirvana Series Book 1)
Copyright 2015 by J.R. Stewart
ISBN: 978-0-9936397-6-0 All rights reserved
Cover copyright 2015 by Blue Moon Publishers
Cover design: Blue Moon Publishers
Editors: Talia Crockett and Christine Szarmes

Published in Canada by Blue Moon Voices, a division of Blue Moon Publishers, located in Toronto, Canada.

The author greatly appreciates you taking the time to read this work. Please consider leaving a review wherever you bought the book, or telling your friends or blog readers about the Nirvana series, to help spread the word. Thank you for your support.

EPub © Edition October 2015

Printed in Canada

NIRVANA

NIRVANA

J.R. STEWART

BlueMoon
PUBLISHERS

CONTENTS

DEDICATION

*To the early pioneers of Virtual
Reality—you brought us a world
that we are only beginning to
explore.*

THANK YOU

To Adam, Talia, and the whole Blue Moon Publishers team, for your support and belief in this book and the series–you are all a part of this book in many ways.

To Larry, for helping me shape this story in the final hour.

To Chris, for designing a captivating book cover.

To Andy, for creating a stunning book layout.

To a very special group of advance readers. Without your feedback, this book would not be what I have always dreamed of. I cannot thank you enough.

To my mentors who gave me an insight into technology and the Virtual Reality World, as I never thought was possible.

To my mom, for encouraging me to always be true to myself.

PROLOGUE

EIGHT-YEAR-OLD LARISSA Kenders pulls a doll tighter toward her and opens one eye. Crickets call through the screen window and the maple tree casts shadows on the bedroom wall. She watches them for a while, and then, with a few deep sighs, closes her eyes again. After a few minutes, the door creaks open, and she pulls her body tighter around her pillow. The door handle clicks shut and then the mattress of her pink princess bed shifts under the weight of her father's body, his hairy arms reaching for her as he whispers, "Wake up, pretty Larissa."

Her eyes shift over to thirteen-year-old Serge perched on a tree branch as he lowers his camera, and Larissa reaches for a hammer underneath her pillow and slams it down on her father's head. She runs outside in her nightie, her bare feet sliding on the wet grass until she climbs into the treehouse.

"Got the photos?" she asks. Serge shows them to her, and she throws her arms around his neck.

The scene repeats itself, and this time as he whispers, "Wake up, pretty Larissa," seventeen-year-old Larissa Kenders barges through the room, raises her knee, and kicks her leg forward, snapping his body from the bed and onto the ground. He tries to get up and she bashes him again, his body stumbling back to the floor. The moment he raises himself onto his hands, she kicks him three times, till blood pours from his mouth and he collapses.

DR. GURMAN presses "pause" and points proudly to the holographic screen. "This is the healing power of virtual reality. Far better than hypnosis."

"I'm still not convinced." Paloma shakes her head, gold hoops swinging from her ears. Her black hair is slicked back into a short glossy ponytail that sticks out like a pointer's tail.

"As you can see, she's into justice." Gurman starts to replay the scene. "In my professional opinion, Kenders is ideal for the Red Door program."

"Larissa Kenders is a loose cannon." Paloma taps her red heels against the chair.

"She's a musician." Gurman waves her off. "They have their heads in the clouds."

Paloma raises a skeptical eyebrow. "I did further research."

Gurman leans back in his chair to listen. "By the way, don't call her 'Larissa.' She hates it," he says.

Paloma notes the information with an eerie cackle. "We extracted this from her computer diary." Paloma opens her holo-reader, which unfolds a holographic screen that she reads from:

July 14, 2086

Most university pubs are rowdy as it is, but mix that with a punk band that's protesting an animal lab in its very campus, and it's a recipe for disaster. Just what happened a few nights ago.

Two weeks ago, Terk, a senior in the animal rights group, recorded a dead monkey in a cage with a camera they'd planted in one of the labs. Another monkey was curled up in a small cage where it could hardly stretch out, its eye infected, its skin sagging from its ribs and electrodes in its head. They approached Sixty Sextet, and of course, we agreed to support animal liberation.

We had an upcoming gig at a university pub where local media was invited, so the plan was to broadcast the video onto outdoor screens all around the campus about halfway through our concert. Apparently they had some tech whiz freshman student who could fix it so the university couldn't shut down the feed.

I was more excited about this concert than even playing at the Horseshoe. Why? I mean, the Horseshoe has been around for centuries. But when I started the alt-rock four-piece Sixty Sextet, it not only paid for my first year, but it also gave my life meaning. Sure, our stage presence was dominated by our drummer, Lexie, who positioned her drums at the side and straddled her stool the whole time, but we also fought for what we believed in; we had a voice. That night, with Lexie's tight skirts riding up her thighs and her blonde hair whipping around her head when she thrashed the drums, we punctuated lyrics during "Free Me" that became a mantra with the crowd. While I belted out the chorus, Lexie swung her long legs over the stage, signing biceps and ripped abs, and then she handed out stacks of pamphlets that the animal rights group had created. I thought it was a dumb idea, being in a digital age, but a piece of paper was such a novelty that it actually worked. Everyone hung on to them. Until the video started. I saw the tech whiz, Andrew, at the back of the room, queuing up the video. He had come to me earlier to explain how things would work and was sort of shy; I think he might have been a fan. He was actually cute with his freckled face and dimpled chin. My buddy Serge, who was visiting, watched us with a cautious eye, so I just traded numbers to hook up later.

The moment the video started, a riot broke out. Fans protested and security tried to shut things down. They didn't know what was happening until they spotted Andrew in the back. Apparently he had *a reputation, and they put two and two together. Serge shoved them away, but they quickly restrained him. Then Andrew walked up and didn't even know how to throw a punch. I leapt into the mosh pit, ran over the crowd's outstretched arms, and dove straight at the two security guards. No sooner were they down than I yelled at Andrew to run, and then held up a good fight till my fans took over. By that time, one of the guards was wiping blood from his face, and Serge was in a protected corner of the room holding a napkin over his bloody nose. I looked for Andrew in the crowd, but he was gone.*

The next day, the incident was all over the papers. The news broadcast quoted Lexie and I, and ran a video of the riotous crowd superimposed over the video of the monkeys in the background. Overnight, Sixty Sextet became famous. We've been invited to talk shows, and sold an exclusive to a high profile music magazine. We even have an offer to be flown into New York to appear on a late night talk show. I'm going to stop in at Madison Square Garden and catch a concert and make a wish. I still can't believe it's happening.

Paloma looks up at Gurman. "A week later she stormed a mink farm and freed the animals."

"Feisty is good."

Paloma swipes to another page.

"Her statement directly to a journalist on that night was: 'Sixty Sextet supports anyone who inflicts economic sabotage on the people who profit from animal suffering.' She elaborated on this idea to thousands of screaming fans." Paloma taps her red heels against the chair. "She thinks too much."

1

NIRVANA

Madison

"IT WORKED!" Andrew rubs my hands together. "How did it feel?"

Even though a strong pressure is still pushing on my head, I assure him, "Like a cooling sensation running throughout my body. As if someone turned a tap on."

Andrew's use of an implanted, microscopic wireless device that links neural activity directly to electronic circuitry still needs some tweaking. He's always pushing the envelope for this virtual reality system, and he keeps any changes close to his belt until he's completely beta tested everything, so we are the guinea pigs.

Not that I mind—everyone has some kind of nanotechnology in their body—but we are the only ones who have them in our brains. Nanobots are used within circulatory systems to destroy tumours and regulate blood pressure, but Andrew's research takes science beyond medical treatment. Andrew is the head programmer for Nirvana, so he can do things differently. Usually this kind of research would be conducted on lab animals, but that's where my influence has changed his procedures.

"Look at me." His brown eyes search mine. "You can see everything?"

I nod. And then I do a short dance to test every limb, all a part of our startup procedure.

Nirvana is a refuge from the real world, which has growing complications regarding the stability of our environment and life in general, not to mention a crumbling economy and massive unemployment rate. It's Hexagon's virtual reality system, a way they keep the populace placated and appeased while they exert absolute rule and control.

While it's a difficult time in the world for many people, I can still eek out a living as a musician. People need entertainment and an escape, and although we don't have the glitzy concert venues of the past, we still offer music in the dreary concrete halls of bunker complexes.

In Nirvana, however, things are different. Programmers code at a fast pace to recreate the world as it once was. They pull in images, video feeds, and audio to superimpose into a virtual world that feels as real as the one we knew just a few years ago, before the Extinction happened.

Right now, my nanobot produces a virtual image of the screen that is augmented in my field of vision. Eventually, Andrew wants this operating system to be controlled by a person's own thoughts, but for now it's linked to the curved touchscreen on my watch. To the average person it looks like a regular watch, but a small holographic disc on the buckle is my connection between the virtual and real worlds. Ours is a holographic world, with holo-phones, holo-albums, holo-readers; you name it.

We're standing outside of Madison Square Garden on a warm summer evening, with crowds of people pouring out of Penn station, yellow cabs streaming by, and smoke billowing from the hot dog vendor's stand.

"Remember," I say to Andrew, "when we camped out all night to get tickets for that benefit concert?"

Andrew squeezes some mustard on his hot dog and hands it to me. "You vowed you'd play here the next time one was held!"

"That was before the Extinction. There's no Madison Square Garden anymore. Not even New York."

He puts his arm around me and leads me to the front doors of the arena. "Not in Nirvana. Here, everything exists." He stops, and directs my attention to the marquee. "I built this one especially for you."

I look up and see the posters. "Sixty Sextet *Our World* Benefit Concert" towers above a larger-than-life bee symbol in intense colours. On another poster, there's Lexie and I. We're in one of our most famous concert shots: Lexie straddling the drum stool, and me executing my signature dance move with legs splayed out in mid-jump.

"It's a great facade," I say encouragingly.

"Facade?" Andrew's voice holds a tinge of surprise. "I've recreated everything, right down to the 76 Balcony and the iconic Garden ceiling."

He leads me into the Chase Square entrance from 7th Avenue, where previous Sixty Sextet concerts play on the ceiling video screens, and the bee symbol is splattered over an array of merchandise. I stop to look at the t-shirts and sweatshirts, the ball caps and purses, the holo-albums and holo-phone cases. I turn back to Andrew.

"How long did it take you to do this?"

"That's what my late nights were for during the last weeks." His smile reaches from ear to ear at my surprise. "Nothing but the best for my fiancée."

I pick up a concert program. On the back are a number of previous concert images and reviews from the university circuit and smaller venues we had played in Toronto, like the Horseshoe Tavern and the Rivoli:

"Larissa Kenders is one of those raw, expressive musicians whose work makes you feel like an addict. There are not many artists with a voice this vibrant and alive."

"Sixty Sextet seeps into your skin and excites your senses. Their lyrics have bite and a dark beauty that leave you longing for more."

"Lexie has led a charge through the punk community, leaving a vibrant and explosive mark in her path. Her sharp and edgy style will inspire artists for years to come."

I place the program back into the stand. As long as my music is still being heard, that's what matters, but it reaches a smaller audience now with Hexagon exacting so much control. The whole point of our music is the message.

"Thanks, Andrew. I could just stand here forever and take it in."

"You'd disappoint your fans." He points to the lineup forming outside. "It's live," says Andrew. "Old fans. New ones. It's a sold out show."

"In virtual," I confirm.

"Real life," he says with a smile. "They bought tickets to get exclusive access to this virtual concert, and can continue to do so even after tonight. It's a paid experience, and every penny goes to *Our World*. Hexagon has waived all revenue benefits, so one hundred percent goes to your charity." He's trying to read my face, but I'm still in shock. "It's the first virtual concert of its kind, and Sixty Sextet is paving the way."

I can't believe it. My band, here at Madison Square Garden. Here, where Elvis Presley, John Lennon, U2, all the greats through the centuries played.

"When is the concert?"

"Tonight. Makeup's waiting for you backstage. So is Lexie."

I gasp. "She's here?"

Andrew chuckles. "She knew about it all along." He takes my hand and leads me toward the security team. "Happy Birthday, sweetheart."

An hour later, I'm belting out the lyrics to "This Isn't Our World" on a walkway suspended above the crowd and in between three stages. One stage, surrounded by security, is a dance floor that rotates fans from the crowd. A sea of people topple over one another to climb up for one song and grind their bodies to the music. Throughout the whole song, I dance between the two stages to connect with each end of the arena.

For the next song, Lexie straddles the drums in her true fashion while I belt out "Sinkhole," haughtily tossing back my head, fast, cutting, and assured. The searchlights scan over thousands of happily screaming, dancing fans while the camera zooms in on them, projecting their faces on the screens. The crowd is full of teens and preteens, and to my surprise, older adults.

We play through all of our songs, with animated renderings, digital projections, and other effects that Andrew created for me. For our finale, the lights dim and there's only one spotlight on Lexie, with her spare and stirring drumbeat, and another on me. I start into "Honey," a song we haven't played since it was banned by Hexagon, but here in Nirvana, all is possible. A movable catwalk descends, with long screens on either side, running the length of the arena floor and rotating images of our world a decade ago. As the lyrics take us through the Extinction, the images change to show the depleted plant life, the dying animals, the erosion, and then the floods. I can't believe that Andrew has created all of this for me. I walk slowly as if on a funeral march, passing between the screens as through a hallway. In the crowd, lights are flickering, and there isn't one sound until I invite our fans to sing the chorus with us.

"Honey, we still taste you,

Earth, we still need you . . ."

As I head back to the stage, I stop in front of the first screen depicting an image of the current Lake Erie, its lakefront one-sixth of its original size, with dead fish floating on the surface. My silhouette is visible in the projections on the screen, and I hold up my hand in a salute.

"Coho Salmon, we still taste you,

Lake Erie, we still need you."

I turn and gesture to the crowd, and the new chorus is repeated. I continue toward the stage, stopping in front of each screen as it rotates through all of the images. I salute each animal, each natural landscape, with the crowd echoing the chorus, while Lexie builds the drumbeat into a crescendo. Fans storm the dance stage, jumping into the crowd with every salute, turning the floor into the largest mosh pit I've ever seen. Lexie slows down the drumbeat, bringing the crowd back to what's important, and we dim all the lights, with only the images on the screen illuminating the entire stadium.

Then I say, "Never forget. Every one of you . . . we all . . . are punk rockers for the cause that matters." Lexie gives one last drumbeat and we leave the stage.

I still can't believe that Andrew created this gift for me, a stage that worked visually, sonically, and thematically for all of my music. I run backstage to thank him, but he's nowhere to be found.

2

I **WAKE** up in bed, alone. I look around me to get my bearings until I see a familiar photo of Andrew and I on the night table. I'm home. In our bed. I sigh and lay my head back down on the pillow.

When I'm in Nirvana, I don't want to come back here. I've known this green world longer than the desolate one in which we now live, and I'm always hopeful that I'll open my eyes and find out it's been a bad dream. How can plants be gone? How can plentiful food no longer exist? It all happened so quickly that I can still hardly believe it. One summer, trees that had hung heavy with pink peaches or clumps of juicy cherries were empty. In the fall, there wasn't one bright orange pumpkin patch. Then orchards with rows of red apples became only a memory. It was only wheat, rice, and corn that grew, through wind pollination. And pigs were the only livestock left. Sextet wrote songs about it. We led marches and did cross-county tours to save the bees, but nothing helped.

I kick my legs out of bed and slip into my knitted slippers. In a world where everything is so automated, I love the feel of the wool slippers knitted by my grandma when I was a girl. I pad into the dark hallway and toward a slant of light coming from the living room.

Our home is small but comfortable. The dining table is a convertible sphere-shaped cone that opens itself up, pod-like, into a round surface with two seats and a light at the centre; or, the middle section pulls out into a desk with a glowing blue light at the base. Andrew is hunched over the workspace as he usually is, a large holographic screen directly in front of him and our dog Chopper laying at his feet. What a pair: a mixed-breed that was half-starved, and the most valued scientist in Hexagon. He turns when the floor creaks upon my entering.

"How was it?" he asks.

"The usual. A cooling sensation leaving my body."

"The watch is comfortable?"

"Without a doubt." I sit down across from him, and Chopper pads over to nudge his muzzle into my hand. "It's ready, Andrew."

He sighs. "I just need to test a few more things."

"For what?" He's always so cautious when developing new software.

He clicks off his screen and turns to me. "I've come across something."

"You always do. And then you spend months perfecting it."

"Look at all the neurological problems the first headsets caused. If those developers hadn't rushed things . . ."

I wave off the notion. "That was ages ago. Besides, you're using nanobots. They're a medical wonder. There are no side effects."

He just looks off into the distance while Chopper walks back and forth between us, vying for attention.

"Andrew, look at what I just experienced. It was mind-blowing." He's the most confident, brilliant man I know, but the instant he has a breakthrough, he always has these moments of doubt.

"This is different."

"Of course it is. It's not just entertainment; it can be used for educational purposes. Medical. It's limitless."

"That's the problem," he says. The dark circles around his eyes are deeper today, and I'm worried about him.

"You're seeing a problem where there isn't one." I grab his hands. "You always get scared, but this is it. This is the future."

"That's just it." He hangs his head and scratches the backs of Chopper's ears. "Not everyone uses it in the same way."

"Andrew, what's going on?"

"It's huge." He sighs and turns back to his computer. "I'll tell you over coffee tomorrow."

I understand the code. It means we can't talk about it here. Hexagon has surveillance equipment everywhere, even in our private home. We have our own secret language and codes to circumvent that. "I'll tell you over coffee," really means, "I'll tell you in a private place." It has to be a statement that doesn't stand out, but that we know would never be true. Neither of us drinks coffee. I know that, during the day, I'll get more info from him.

It frustrates me, that a person in Andrew's position is still subjected to this kind of scrutiny. But, if you're not a board member or stakeholder, you don't count in Hexagon's world.

I remove the steel-grey leather band and return the watch to him. "Did you see the concert?"

He nods.

"All of it? Were you there?"

He turns to me, his eyes sunken. "You know I never lie to you." He rubs his eyes. "I saw your first song, but I had to come back here."

"You didn't see it live?"

"I'll watch it on replay."

I sink into the chair next to him. "It felt live to me."

"It's supposed to." He reaches out his hands. "I wanted you to have a birthday you'll never forget."

"I won't ever."

"Good."

"Are you coming to bed?"

"I want to. I really do."

I wave him off. "I understand."

But do I? I get the creative process. I take the same approach when writing a song. I don't talk about it, I don't share it, not until it's done.

Andrew and I are similar that way. We're music and science. It's creation and invention; writing a melody or an equation, conceiving new lyrics or a theory. So I give him a brief shoulder rub and head into the kitchen to make him a midnight snack. When I come back to the room, however, he's shaking his head and muttering to himself. Whatever he's stumbled upon, it's not all good.

3

THE SHRILL five a.m. siren jolts me awake to the usual calamity. The bunker's stale air; the pelting of dust balls and stray debris. I groan and hear Andrew's chuckle. When I open my eyes, he's getting dressed.

"Are you leaving already?" I ask.

Andrew leans down for one long kiss. "It's eight o'clock."

I bolt up in bed. "The five a.m. just went off."

"Nope. You slept through that one."

I groan. "I'm late."

He leans over me. "You always are, Kenders."

I rub my eyes. "When will you be home?"

"Late. I've got a meeting with my boss."

I let out a long yawn. "Cheating on me again?" I wink.

He laughs and pulls out my photo from his breast pocket. "I've got this framed on my desk."

"You should get a better picture."

"The green dress matches your eyes."

I turn up my nose. "My grad photo is outdated."

"It says everything about you. No one dictates what Kenders does. You wouldn't wear school colours like the rest of the class did. Your green dress stood out, just like you do."

He's right. Our punk band was protesting the loss of habitat for bees, and this wardrobe choice was one of many anti-establishment statements we made that year. Since 2080, when Hexagon became the university's major sponsor, it had been a new tradition to wear school colours. We boycotted that convention, and even at graduation we were handing out flyers, standing up for what we believed in.

Andrew kisses me on the lips. "I'll see you at lunch."

About an hour later, I wake up to a softer buzzing. This time, Andrew has set the alarm for me. He knows me well enough to be sure that I'll drift back to sleep the moment he leaves. I jump out of bed to get ready. I run a comb through my tangled bangs, and pull up a mat of brown hair, covered in dust. That's what happens when you hit the shower too late: no water in the reservoir, not even enough to brush my teeth. I rub at the dark splotches of dirt until my pale skin turns bright pink, and then give up on my hair and pull it into a ponytail while I step into my uniform. I stop for a moment before heading out the door, and pull Andrew's sweatshirt over my head. It drapes in a large fold over my narrow shoulders. I rush to jump onto the bus rumbling down the road, but it's already passed by my compound.

That's me. Always late. I can hear Mom's voice in my head: "Your friends have full-time jobs. They're already paying off their student loans. And look at you, playing in bars. You're good at math and science. Be an accountant. A teacher."

Thanks, Mom. Way back in high school she already objected. If I had a jazz band she would have approved, but she couldn't relate to punk. As if punk wouldn't pay the bills.

She was right, but I didn't tell her that at the time.

Mom never forgave me for dumping my scholarship, but I was fourteen. To this day, she can't understand that I'd had enough of classical music lessons. Piano lessons every night since I was five. Then violin. I refused a wind instrument. She wanted to turn me into a child prodigy, and I just wanted to be normal. In high school that meant getting poor grades so I wouldn't stand out. I had a deal with my math teacher: single me out in class with a question, and I'd flunk the exam on purpose. So he left me alone in the back of the room, and all through the lessons I daydreamed and wrote songs.

It was harder to avoid being pegged in university with a scholarship, so I dropped it after first year and ramped up Sextet. Freedom at fifteen! Gone was the ironed shirt I had to wear for concert band. Without the scholarship, I could choose my own classes. When I dyed my hair, Mom thought I had joined some religious cult and said she had lost her baby.

I couldn't understand why Mom was so possessive. I mean, I know things didn't work out with my dad, but don't turn me into a trophy just because you married a drunk. The more she imposed rules at home, and the more flack I got for being lazy and careless and full of anger, the more I rebelled with shorter skirts and ripped shirts. If she wouldn't bother listening to my lyrics, if she didn't know that punk stood for peace and not hate, then I was done living under Totalitarianism. Punks don't take orders. Punks take action, so I packed my bags and moved in with my band members.

Even when Sixty Sextet became the opening act, even when we formed a peace march, even when we stormed a factory farm and freed a thousand chickens from their wire cages in a windowless barn, all Mom did was repeat the same message: "Get a good job. One that gives you a pension."

Newsflash, Mom, wherever you are: pensions don't exist anymore. Not with Hexagon.

I walk along the road, cough with my first breath, then pull on my mask. The air is thicker than usual, and it stings my lungs. This isn't what I thought my life would be at seventeen. How did we mess up the earth this much? A hundred years ago, in 1987, an international treaty was signed in Montreal for a fifty percent reduction in the use of CFCs by the year 2000. While they were worried then about destroying the ozone layer, I bet they never thought that the loss of bees, right here on the planet, would cause such havoc.

After the loss of bees came the depletion of plant life. Then trees were uprooted and erosion occurred, causing windstorms and then droughts. Hexagon siphoned off the little water that was left for themselves and channeled it into their dikes toward their food production region, the Farm, and then to the rich in the Bubble. They couldn't care less about everyone else.

Now Hexagon controls everything. They're the massive corporation that touts themselves as saving the day after the economy and government tanked. While they paint a picture of providing a refuge for survivors who flooded into their open arms, the truth is they offered no other alternative. I'm considered a lucky one to work at Hexagon headquarters, a high walled compound that covers thousands of acres. Lucky is a four hundred-square-foot bunker space; Andrew and I get double the size because we're a couple, and, because he's a top progammer we're on the main floor with a small patch of green they call a backyard.

More than thirty thousand people are crammed into these quarters, while the remaining acreage is for the greedy Hexagon executives. Hexagon Estate homes are mansions spread over fake grass and recirculating water. Even though it sounds grand, the Hexagon employees who live there don't feel privileged. They'd rather be at the Bubble.

Of course, I don't have access to the estates, but I work in the coveted space, the one building that covers ten acres: Nirvana. It houses the only source of pleasure and connection to Earth before the Extinction that any of us have. Its servers are kept in a secret location, but the pleasure dome is right here at Hexagon.

At nine o'clock I enter the Nirvana complex to relieve Terk, who held down the midnight shift. It's the only white building in the entire compound, with crystal chandeliers and iridescent glass tiled walls in the lobby. The waiting room is covered with a creamy plush carpet and white silk wall coverings that arc toward the frosted glass door that opens to the individual pods. The actual pods themselves are very small, and would be claustrophobic if it wasn't for the comfortable seat and the steady pressure from a headset. Most people stop caring what their real world looks like the moment they enter Nirvana.

I notice the latest Nirvana Escape poster. The tagline, "Who can you be in Nirvana?" invites users to upload their own personal stories as a signature experience. They cycle through these marketing campaigns each quarter, and people go Nirvana crazy. Last quarter it was "Your Best Dream," encouraging people to spend an entire night in Nirvana.

I prefer the quiet pace of the night shift. I feel like a nurse applying virtual intravenous; you hook them up and they're out for ten hours. And really, Nirvana is better than anxiety meds or sleeping pills. When the Extinction hit, people were distressed, scared, and nervous. For more than half their pay, fifteen minutes in Nirvana is the balm that works. You feel the pressure as an ear piece is pulled over your hair and cups each side of your skull, and then a minute later the weightless, spongy sensation of your head as you enter a world where anything is possible.

While Nirvana is very much Andrew's creation, he'd prefer if people didn't spend their money on fifteen minutes in Nirvana, and rather they save their earnings instead.

"For what?" I always say. "They could never afford the Bubble."

"There's a future," is his standard answer.

If there's one thing I appreciate about Andrew, it's that he clings to hope. Always. I'm more of a realist in that regard.

"There's nothing beyond Hexagon," I always say.

He disagrees, but it's a moot point anyway. I think Hexagon uses Nirvana to track us, and listen to our thoughts and conversations. People usually get so caught up with their fantasies in there that they forget the regimented world we live in. A virtual reality experience isn't someone's private show.

I'm well aware of what really goes on because I'm always the one who presses the record button once they're in. I'm the one who registers the analysis algorithm. I never know what's discussed, and all I can do is remove their headset, record their obligatory Nirvana visit into the system, and say, "Enjoy the day."

Every so often, though, when I take off a headset a red light flashes, which means I should check "Red" on the digital form before me. It's Hexagon's new Red Door program, and it's known among operators that "Reds" are never seen again. We don't know what happens to them, but we know it's not good. One day, one of the operators didn't report a Red, and we never saw him again, either.

Terk and I have a pact that we do not report a Red. Rather, we tell Andrew, who can re-code that person's profile. It has to be done within twenty-four hours, and we have our secret language for letting him know. It takes time for Andrew to do this, and because he can't trust anyone else on his team, he does it late at night in the lab. He tells Tremaine that he's working on more developments for Nirvana, then often comes under fire for the slow progress. Tremaine is Hexagon's head honcho, and Nirvana has become his pet project, much to Andrew's dismay. Tremaine's vision doesn't align with Andrew's. Sooner or later, there will be a system in place to monitor the Red Door, but for now, we can save people every day.

These small victories are all we have until someone, something, can take Tremaine down.

I hand Terk a muffin. "Thanks for covering."

He lifts his chin from the palm of his hand, looks up at me, and lowers his elbow from the moulded desk to make room. "No problem. I owe you one."

He owes me a ton, but who's counting among friends. Terk and I go way back to the activism days. In fact, he was the leader of an animal rights group at university, and is the one who introduced Andrew and I.

Although I still consider myself a musician, I'm a pod operator here at Hexagon. My main job is to operate one station consisting of four pods and one super pod. Most people stay in Nirvana for fifteen minutes, so it's busy work cycling all of them through every hour. If couples go into the virtual world together, they can spread their time to half an hour, an absolute luxury that most couldn't afford.

For the most part, I control the pods from the station. We can monitor any activity within Nirvana from the console, but there isn't much time for it. Our main concentration is on the super pod, which is reserved for Hexagon board members only.

"Anything exciting happen?" I ask Terk. A slight smile crosses his face.

"Just Tremaine in with his usual sex forays. Apparently he had such a good time, he'll be back for a short break at ten a.m."

Terk is the quiet one whom most people overlook. He prefers to keep a low profile and do his work underneath the radar.

"Ugh." I place the headset over his dark hair, braided close to his scalp in complex geometric and curved patterns. He closes his eyes, and for the first time I notice that his thin goatee bears the first splashes of grey. As operators, we need to take a mandatory fifteen minutes once a week. It's considered a luxury, and Terk doesn't mind, but to me, it's creepy. I feel like I'm being watched.

Before Andrew started developing Nirvana, we'd go in together. That's what we have our secret language for. While some selected wild adventures, we were careful to stay in an area where we wouldn't lose sight of where we were, and chose pleasant walks through meadows. We used to explore Nirvana even more, and had tried everything: swam in the ocean with gills and fins as whales, scuttled along the earth as ten-foot-tall giants with eight legs, performed aerial dances like those we had often watched together in circus shows. That's how it is in this virtual reality world: always exciting and magical.

Some colleagues choose to spend their time in Nirvana exploring imaginary worlds or learning to fly like the birds. My former band members hang out at punk concerts. These activities interested me before, but since the Red Door, we always choose Earth, and say something complimentary about Hexagon each time we're under watch in the system. Anything and everything is possible in Nirvana, but Earth is the safe place. I'm certain of it. Each time we run our fingers down the list of possibilities—skydiving, caving, rock climbing, scuba diving—we swipe the screen until "soft adventure" appears and then select "apple orchard" in that section.

By the time I've reminisced on some of my favourite Nirvana experiences, the buzzer has gone off for Terk's fifteen minutes. As I remove his headset, out of the corner of my eye, I see the red light flash. I can't believe it, and deliberately stumble, enough to kick the light cord out. I don't want this signal to ever be spotted in any records.

My heart is still pumping when I look up at him and say, "Enjoy the day." As I enter my second incorrect recording into the system for this week, I wonder how much longer we can do this before we're found out. Andrew says Hexagon would never do anything to hurt me because they need him, but can he protect me forever? As Terk tells me, these aren't the animal farms I raided as a student–the stakes are much higher.

I smile back at Terk as he leaves, my insides still shaking. If I were found out, I'd be in the Red Door, or even killed for treason.

4

TREMAINE RESTS his bony shoulders against the seat, and I pull the headset over his ears. He doesn't even look at me; I'm beneath him, a mindless operator just pushing buttons. It doesn't matter that I am a rock star with a big fan base. It's that way for the digitally immortal: they can't relate to human beings anymore. We have weak biological bodies that falter and fail, while theirs are powerful and limitless.

Everyone who lives in the Bubble has uploaded their entire mind to a computer. Keeping their digital selves alive is the cornerstone of Hexagon's cashflow. They operate the Bubble and cater to the biological whims of each human, but they have an evergreen revenue stream with the digitally immortal.

Even a fascist dictatorship has bills to pay and graft to finance.

Even if I had the money, I wouldn't upload my entire mind to a computer and replace my human body with mechanical parts. I wouldn't want my songs-in-progress to be accessed by some jazz musician and changed to a standard four/four ride pattern. It would be like those unfinished Mozart manuscripts that were uncovered in Austria during the Extinction, when that rap artist misinterpreted them. Some things are meant to live and die with an artist.

Tremaine moans in his chair, and I know he's found his blonde. That's all he ever comes here for. Another conquest, an orgy, a three-some. He's creepy. I wonder what tycoons like him did a century ago when all they had was a virtual picture on a screen. They thought they were hot stuff then, just like Tremaine thinks he is now.

And then there's me. The average lifespan in our current environment is forty years for men and forty-seven years for women, so I've got another thirty years. At this point, I don't even know what that means. Corporal keeps telling me I'll change my mind about digital immortality once I push forty. "You'll feel old, then," he tells me. "Your body will start wearing out." Corporal has known me since I was a child and is a replacement father. Forty seems like a lifetime away; I can't even imagine twenty at this point.

I don't have any close friends who are digital immortals, but apparently, it's hard to tell them apart. Nano technology is so advanced now that the non-biological bodies are very convincing. It makes sense. If we can create virtual reality and virtual bodies that are as life-like as the real thing, why can't we reverse that for our physical world, too?

Call me old-fashioned, but I like the physical world. I trust it more. There are certain things I won't digitize, and my music is one of them. I only put my notes on paper. Music, to me, is way too personal.

In an hour, an alarm sounds, which mutes the music I'm playing. It's time for me to program an experience into Nirvana, and I walk over to Tremaine's pod. He has a pre-selection built in; personal choices just for him. I look down at his pathetic body. The wiry mouth, the crooked finger, the thin hair pasted to his forehead. It's masked by his designer clothes, but when you sit for hours looking at someone, you see past all of that. This is how I spend my time. Looking at fools.

To my surprise, his selection is for Lexie. It feels odd for me to pro-gram Lexie into his virtual reality experience, but I just push the button and the computer pulls her data from live feeds, simulating her voice and body movements into different scenarios for Tremaine's pleasure.

At noon, Andrew slumps down in the chair next to me with lunch.

He's the only one who can get access anywhere in this building, and it's our usual ritual, even if he can only stay for ten minutes.

"How many hours is Tremaine in for?"

"The usual." I need to tell Andrew about Terk's Red Door. I need to warn him. "How long are you here for?" I wink.

"Two minutes. I've got a golf game with Tremaine and the board in two hours, and I need to prep. I'll be peppered with questions, as usual."

"Make sure you let Tremaine win."

"Everyone always does."

While I program Tremaine's next experience, Andrew pulls out his holo-phone and sends a message. I glance over at the screen, expecting it to be a secret message to me, but all I see are the words: "We need to talk, off-site."

I wonder if this message has to do with his apprehension the other night. At times, I feel like Hexagon owns him because of Nirvana. It's no different for regular working people, either; ones who can't afford more than fifteen minutes a week, and end up trading their work pay for time in Nirvana. Hexagon owns us forever, work-wise, too. Sometimes I wonder where Hexagon makes more of their money: in Nirvana, or through food production at the Farm where workers toil under harsh conditions to provide nourishment to the general population.

"When are we having coffee?" I ask. I want to tell him about Terk, and I want to know what Andrew's problems are. I've been feeling a weight descending on our lives and closing in on us that I don't like.

"Tomorrow," he says, and is off with a quick kiss. I hand him a folded paper with our cryptogram buried on the second line of one of my music sheets. It's a complex system of symbols for twenty-four letters, and the letters are formed by using five different pitches and altering the stem directions and note values. We used the cryptograms during our social activism days for meet ups. In those days, we placed them on everything. Napkins. Our hands. It was our own secret language; we never thought we'd live in a system where we'd use them in our everyday life.

The decoded notes spell, "Red: Terk." Andrew knows what to do.

5

ANDREW

Hexagon

ANDREW WATCHES Tremaine bend down to the golf ball, his large stomach folding over his pants and hanging like a sac. *What a loser,* he thinks.

He goes through his habitual routine, measuring the right distance from the ball before each swing, then checking the angle. "A device in your head eliminating the need for a screen?" The group of four lean on their clubs and wait. There are days when the entire board comes out to play; when it's Tremaine's course, he changes all the conventional rules of the game.

Andrew bends down so they're at eye level. "Directly into your field of vision."

Corporal presses his bushy eyebrows together. "We'll really become androids."

"For the first time, human brains will be merged with computer intelligence," says Andrew with excitement. "People can experience virtual reality from within their own nervous systems."

"You can't digitize instinct." Corporal grits his crooked front teeth. "Or emotion." He taps his club. "We rely on that as security, don't we, Paloma?"

Paloma pushes her cropped black hair away from her blanched face. She looks from Corporal to Tremaine and then back. "Yes sir," is all she can say.

With a slight wave of his hand, Tremaine motions to Serge, and all heads turn. "What does our major stakeholder think?"

"It's like an extension of your mind." Serge runs his hands through his tousled hair, in awe of the concept. "This is monumental."

Tremaine casts a doubtful look at Serge, Paloma, and Andrew, then smiles at Corporal in a knowing fashion.

"I love playing on a real course." He turns toward the robotic caddy and grabs another club. "Do you know that I never play in Nirvana? I built an outside course instead."

Andrew's palms suddenly become sweaty, and he switches the club to his other hand. The last time Tremaine told this story, he cut funding to his lab, and Andrew had to let two people go. Tremaine prides himself on his golf game as much as he does his business investments; he wants to be in complete physical control of what he's doing.

Tremaine positions himself for another swing. "I took the best pilot and flew over the dunes, following the natural terrain, to find the best site." He looks up at Andrew. "Just like you. The star programmer, the young hopeful."

He hits the ball with a knockdown swing. "We laid down a patch of fake grass here on the best site, and created this nine-hole course." He watches the ball glide low, then turns to Andrew. "We've invested a ton of money into this so far."

Everyone glares at Andrew, especially Paloma with her steel-grey eyes. "Four years to be exact," she says.

Andrew wonders if she has an agenda beyond sheer revenge, and turns to address her. "We've made significant breakthroughs."

Tremaine pauses for a moment, his pressed shirt stretching over his stomach. "But not one that we can monetize yet."

Andrew looks at each of the disapproving faces; they're all ganging up on him. He expects it from Paloma. Any chance she gets, she's on the attack. She doesn't know where to draw the line. Last fall, when she killed Kenders' cat, he threatened her, and rather than be taken aback, she laughed in his face.

Now that she's on security, the power has gone to her head. What Andrew saw in her he'll never understand, but he's grateful he didn't put a ring on her finger.

Andrew's attention is drawn to Corporal, who's muttering something under his breath at Serge.

"You know I have to conduct research that is free of corporate interests," Andrew insists. "That was our agreement." Thank goodness there are only four board members he has to answer to this time.

Andrew believes in his work, and tries to convince members of the group as to the necessity of thorough research, and the importance of considering longterm medical and societal impacts. He sees his job as no different from his academic years spent defending theories and hypotheses. He won't stop insisting on his ideals, even when browbeaten by the menacing Tremaine. It's discouraging, though, as more and more he feels as if he's part of an academic clique whose members build their careers on fear-mongering over the Extinction and ensuing threats, rather than on finding actionable solutions. The group identity is formed around threats of hunger, riots, and more environmental disasters, which bolsters their careers, rather than a collective interest in improving life on Earth. Andrew observes all of this from a close distance, and questions the relevance of their circle and the supposed threats.

"Let's be clear." Tremaine rubs his hands together. "Public science in the public interest doesn't exist anymore."

Andrew has nothing to say. He's spent enough time in academia throughout his career to notice Hexagon's corporate branding appearing on everything from lecture halls to research chairs. To him, it was a sellout, and as a researcher he is now a part of it. He knows of programs that promoted the causes of their corporate funders in published papers. He vowed never to do that, and now here he is, playing golf with the very people who constantly ask him to compromise his integrity. If

Kenders knew, she'd tell him to walk, but how can he abandon everything he's spent a lifetime to learn? And, something that could have a monumental effect on people suffering from challenges, such as blindness or acrophobia.

Tremaine steps aside as Paloma walks up with her club.

"What did you expect after the Extinction? You should be grateful your funding wasn't cut when public tax dollars ended. We stepped in for you," Tremaine says as he pats Andrew on the back. "And this has huge revenue potential." He turns to the rest of the group. "Porn. Gambling. Andrew, you're going to make us a fortune."

Every face turns to look at Andrew, and he does his best to force a smile. Revenue is not his intention with the research. He sees advances for medical science, and educational training, not this. All the while, Tremaine is still spewing off possibilities, right down to his own fantasy of seeing a hot blonde while he's on top of his wife.

Paloma swings, then watches Tremaine's reaction as the ball lands.

"How do these nanobots enter the body?" she asks.

"They're microscopic, and are guided toward the neurons in the brain responsible for visual, auditory, and other senses. When a person wants to experience a simulated reality, the nanobots move into place, suppress input from the real senses, and replace them with signals for the virtual environment."

"What safety measures do you have in place?"

"The nanobot detaches itself from a neuron when there is a power shut off, and a person is automatically returned to the real world." He won't tell them about the watch that controls it. That technology he will only give them when he can completely trust their intentions.

"So you can't get trapped in a virtual environment?" Paloma suddenly looks concerned, as if she knows something that no one else does.

"Definitely not. They can be removed at any time."

"If we want them to be." Tremaine starts to pace. "It gives us a whole other angle on surveillance and monitoring." He looks at Paloma, and she nods. "We now have control over food production, but there's so much more." He looks at Andrew. "We need to roll this out."

Andrew reaches for his club, holding back the urge to swing it at Tremaine. He's staring into the eyes of the commercialization of academia.

"I can't give you a timeline yet."

Tremaine dismisses Andrew's statement with a wave of his hand. "We've heard this for too many years. You're in there night and day. Don't look surprised. We have logs. We know what you're up to."

Andrew sets down his ball, but has no desire to even swing the club. Golf is a game that heralds honesty, honour, and respect; it's not just hitting a ball along grassy terrain. This sport has become a competition, just as Nirvana is a contest for individual members of Hexagon's board. Years ago, Tremaine denied the university the right to publish Andrew's findings, because they weren't favourable to Hexagon. His career is always being put on hold by them. But now, what choice does he have? He doesn't have the funds to go private.

Tremaine waits impatiently, with his hands on his hips. "We want a full report, then. Itemizing everything you're doing and why. We haven't asked that from you for years, but our researchers in food production are constantly submitting. It's time you started."

Andrew places his hands out in front of the club. "It will slow production time down."

Tremaine chuckles, then says dryly, "Then get your bankroll elsewhere." He hands his club to the caddy and taps Andrew on the shoulder with an evil smile. "Let's be clear. Your lab shuts down tomorrow if we cut the funding. You're a superstar programmer because we made you that. We put you on the front page of the papers. We send you to conferences. We fund your book."

Andrew takes a hard swing and misses the ball. "This research takes time."

"Then test it on monkeys. Speed up the process." He starts to walk away, and says over his shoulder, "You have two days."

AS CORPORAL and Andrew walk down to the next golf hole, Tremaine and Serge stop Paloma. "Make sure you stay on Andrew," orders Tremaine. "If virtual reality can switch to full immersion, we'll make a fortune. Stakeholders like Serge, here, need to see profit margins rise."

"If you push him too far, he'll stop the research like last time," Paloma replies. She knows this fact too well. Five years ago, Tremaine prodded her to push Andrew, and he dumped her. She didn't deserve to be dropped like that; to be told that it was over, and cancel out five years. How could he humiliate her? Disappoint her? She had tried to get him back, but all her attempts had failed.

Tremaine folds his arms. "Then push without him knowing it."

Paloma knows she is the only one who truly understands Andrew. She knew him before Kenders, before anyone was aware of Andrew's brilliant mind.

"He's too smart for that."

Tremaine shuffles his feet impatiently. "He's got to drop his ethics. We had seats on the university's advisory board for years before he came on the scene, and we always influenced programming. He's working for a corporation now, not a university."

Paloma nods with certainty. "His academic days are over." And there's more she wishes could be over with him. That relationship with the musician, for starters. He was a professional; what was he doing being seen with a punker? It *will* be over, if she can help it. She thought it would be enough to drown Kenders' cat. Shouldn't that have sent the message that she wouldn't be overlooked? All it did, though, was cast the foul-mouthed punker straight into Andrew's arms, and he caved. He's grown too soft.

"It's critical that this happens. Corporal doesn't need to know about it. Come to me directly," Tremaine insists.

Paloma sighs. She was the one who introduced Andrew to Hexagon, and look where he is now: at the top of their research facility, with a complete disregard for her. Did he once even acknowledge her in the group today? No. Did he give her the slightest smile? No.

She is done with being nice to him. She will hit him where it counts: Kenders.

"If you convince him, Paloma," Serge says, "you'll get a percentage of Nirvana."

6

NIRVANA

Training

WE'RE IN the back of a truck as it rumbles down a rough road. Corporal calls out instructions to security trainees so loudly that veins bulge from his neck. From the long scar across his pocked cheek to the wide galaxy tattoo on his shoulder, he's scary-looking as it is without the shouting. Each person on the bench wears navy cargo pants, a matching crew t-shirt, and polished brown combat boots laced up above the ankles.

"They don't call me 'Corporal' for nothing. I've been in more real wars and reconnaissance missions than you boys have played in video games." He starts pacing up and down the aisle. "Today is your final test in ground security. Terrorists have taken over the building. Board members are trapped on the penthouse level. We're searching every floor to rid ourselves of these bastards. No questions. Shoot to kill. It's not a game, boys. Fuck up and you're out. Make the right moves, and you're on to round three of being on Hexagon's A-list team."

Even though Corporal's speech didn't address the two women in the group, I can see the fear in each person's eyes as they file out of the truck and fall in behind Corporal. They dread their realities if they don't make this cut: slopping mud at a pig farm in the Farm region.

They've been living on four hours of sleep a night, and the training intensifies every day; breaching walls and drown-proofing are only two of the tasks that lie ahead. Only twenty-five percent of those who apply make it to the Hexagon academy each year. Corporal puts them through the rigours as if they're going into a World War, but the graduates will mostly end up protecting dignitaries and Hexagon board members.

I'm the sweep, pressing through the thick brush behind a trail of broken twigs the group has blazed for me. In the clearing, the five-storey building sits on top of a limestone cliff, and the first eager trainees are already scaling it. I follow the edge of the forest till I find a well-worn path, and lean against the wall in the morning sun while, one by one, faces gleaming with sweat crest the hill. Corporal scowls when he sees me standing there.

The funny thing is, Corporal always wants a VR operator with him when he's in Nirvana; he doesn't trust the system. He's a hands-on, non-immersive kind of guy, and the virtual world is something he can't wrap his head around. Put him on the real ground, and he'll face anything; he has enough scars to prove it. But in Nirvana, he's uneasy. For a guy who makes every burly cadet hopeful tremble, I'm his security blanket on routine training in Nirvana. This admission alone has put Corporal into a vulnerable state with me. It is our secret. But then, we have many. My father Frank took a bullet for him when they were in the military decades ago. Frank took to drinking, and Corporal always felt responsible. Each month, he sent money to my mother.

While Corporal doesn't want virtual reality training, Tremaine insisted, because all actions and communications are recorded and replayed for review. This new training regime is more about Tremaine wanting to control everything than anything else. Nothing falls under the Hexagon radar. Say the wrong word, and it's the Red Door.

The trainees are lightning quick as they move through the door and spread out to secure the target building. We work from the top down in multi-storey buildings, and I lead the way while Corporal pulls security on the perimeter. While I don't have security or military training, I have ambushed more places than any of the other VR operators, even if they were unethical animal farms, so I was Corporal's first choice.

Within two minutes, two trainees are already heading to the truck. Listening closely to orders, as basic as it sounds, is a critical training element, and becomes difficult when brains get tired from lack of sleep. Corporal purposely left out part of an order to see who was really listening. These two didn't even make it into the building.

I watch CJ; he's carrying the recoilless, ready to shoot through a wall if he needs to. He takes down two infiltrators with precision, but I know what's waiting for him behind the next door. As much as Corporal hates the virtual reality training ground, there are certain learning skills you can't simulate otherwise, and explosives is one of them. Back in the day, Corporal trained in shoot-houses where he'd watch and critique from a catwalk above the rooms. When he spent days at the Nirvana console, watching the trainees and making notes while slugging down mugs of coffee, he came up with the idea of planting bombs that could detonate, again and again, without any building damage. It was a challenge for Andrew's team. While they had coded in additional soldiers, typed in real-time conversations, and dropped in an enemy for a counterattack, planting and timing bombs was more difficult to simulate.

I hear, "Shit," and I know CJ has found the bomb. I move away in anticipation of an explosion and wait. I count seconds, and then an ear-splitting blast knocks me off my feet. *Damn, Andrew's team is good.* CJ was the last one of the day; three trainees are removed from today's session as the team dwindles down to fifteen in numbers.

I stay at the top, waiting for Corporal's signal to descend, and walk into the sun filtering through the window.

I hear a sound behind me, and spin around as a figure walks out of the shadows. I pull out the weapon I'm forced to carry, aim hastily, and shoot. He doesn't drop, but rather looks up at me with a big smile. It's Andrew.

I do a double take, and he winks.

"Just wanted to tell you I forgot to change Chopper's water bowl."

Just like that, he's gone, and I hear Corporal approaching, taking two stairs at a time. "Kenders, what the hell?" He's at the top of the stairs. "Who'd you kill? We're done."

"I . . . I thought I saw someone." I'm waiting for the pressure on my head, for the headset to save me from this embarrassment.

7

"WHAT WERE you doing in VR training?"

Andrew chuckles. "I missed you."

"You freaked me out."

"I was trying something new."

"You made me look stupid. No one saw you but me."

He comes to my side. "I know." His voice is sincere and calm, but I still glare at him.

"How did you do that?"

"I can appear for a few seconds before being spotted." He presses his eyebrows together like he always does when he's worried, and in a tender voice says, "This way, I can look out for you."

I swallow any anger. I know he's worried about something, I just can't tell what. I reach out for him and run my finger along his strong jaw, then over his lips. He kisses me, and then lowers his body onto mine. Our limbs are entwined when a bright light from his computer illuminates the darkened room. He stops for a moment, and I can see the tension in his face.

This isn't the way I want it, and I release my hands from his. "Is it work?"

He nods.

"Is something wrong?"

"I can't tell you."

"They work you too hard. Expect too much . . ."

"It's not that." He rubs my shoulders. "I'll work it out."

"Can I help?"

"Don't worry about it."

The next morning, I wake up late and to an empty bed, but Andrew has left breakfast on the night table. Obedient Chopper sits next to it, licking his lips, patiently waiting for his treat. I break off a piece of bread; he knows what's coming and gets up on all fours, wiggling his back legs with excitement. It's my day off, so I linger in bed, sharing my breakfast with Chopper.

I call Andrew on his holo-phone, but he doesn't answer. I call the lab next, and they tell me that he never came to work. I call Nirvana headquarters, and Terk says he hasn't come by for the routine weekly check.

I slump into my chair, trying to figure out what happened. Andrew has been tense and worried for days; now I wonder if he's in some kind of trouble.

Chopper rests his head on my knee, and I knuckle between his ears. "And you thought your life was chaos when we rescued you from that farm!" I plant a kiss on his muzzle. "Look what you're into with us now." I bend my head down and rest it on his. His warm tongue licks my fingers, and it calms me. The rescued, now safeguarding me.

As I'm lying there, I feel a vibration on my arm, and my watch boots up. I snap upright and look at the curved touchscreen. Nirvana opens on its own, without me powering in, and Chopper whimpers as I start to tremble.

8

NIRVANA

Reboot

I FEEL the familiar cooling sensation enter my body without even pressing a button. Immediately I'm in the apple orchard, and I spin around to get my bearings.

I lean against a tree and take shallow breaths. Questions flood my mind as I set my feet onto the stone-dust trail. I need to talk to Andrew again. What kind of trouble is he in? I'm resourceful, but if his problems are work related, I've never been up against the likes of Hexagon.

Nothing like this. This is real.

Andrew grabs ahold of my shoulders, and I press him away at arm's length. "Don't boot me in like that. Scares the hell out of me!"

"Sorry. I had no choice."

"You're okay?"

He runs his hands along my face. "Don't worry. I can't speak now, I only have a few seconds."

"Why? What's happening?"

He rubs my shoulder. "Trust no one. Not even Serge."

"Are you in trouble?"

"Lay low, and make sure your watch stays with you. Wear it wherever you go."

I nod. "I'm scared for . . ."

"I love you." His voice is despondent, his eyes sullen, and then the cooling sensation leaves my body.

9

I'M BACK in my room. I stare at the wall for a long time, hoping Andrew will come back to me, but the watch is black and lifeless. It's a prototype, and I have no clue how it works. Someone bangs on my door but I ignore them, continuing to stare at the wall, and trying to figure out what just happened.

Chopper won't stop his barking at the persistent knocking, so eventually I open the door. A tall woman with cropped black hair blocks the doorway. "Where's Andrew?"

"He isn't here."

"When did he leave?"

I size up the crow's feet on her round face, the simple band on her stubby finger, and figure she's the same age as my mother. Both exude blatant disregard for the younger generation.

"I don't know."

"Where's his computer?"

She steps into the doorway, but I block her. "What is this about?" I demand.

Her eyes are like smoke, and stone cold. "We need to see his files."

"Do you have a warrant?" I ask, distracted by Chopper's growling as he stands next to my leg.

"We don't need one." She pushes past me with a thug flanking her, and struts into the room. Chopper bares his teeth, and with one quick flick of her hand she restrains him with a rope. I lunge at her, but the thug holds me back while she drags my dog to the bedroom and closes the door.

"Relax, he's not hurt." Her voice is hard and cold.

I yank one arm free and lunge again, but her fingers wrap around mine before I can even come close to her face. She clamps down hard, but looks surprised at my attack. *You haven't seen anything yet.*

"One more step and I'll call security," I threaten. They don't scare me.

She's wearing a white shirt tucked into a pencil skirt, and she flashes a badge along with her thug. The name "Paloma" is all I see before she closes it.

"I am security," she snarls.

"I want to hear it from Corporal."

"He's detained elsewhere," she snaps back.

She towers over me in her heels, but I stand my ground, my eyes piercing through hers.

"Andrew will file a complaint when he gets home."

She sneers at me. "Andrew is gone."

"What?"

It can't be. I talked with him just hours ago in Nirvana. Was that real?

She starts to sift through his desk. "His workstation and his files have been destroyed, and . . ."

I push her away, but she twists my arm and shoves me against the wall.

"You have no idea who you're messing with," she hisses as she presses hard against my ribs. Dark eyeliner accentuates her angry grey eyes. "Now, where is his computer?"

"I . . . I don't know," I stammer. I collect myself, and try to calm my nerves. I won't let her know she's getting under my skin.

"His life could be at risk, and you won't help us."

"Why is he in danger?" I don't get the warm fuzzy notion that she cares about him.

"It's confidential."

I snap back, "So are the whereabouts of his computer."

I can smell the garlic on her breath. Her pallid face is now inches from mine as she sneers, "One last time."

My heart is pounding, but I won't let her feel it. I've been in police face-offs when we did stand-ins at animal farms, and I've been interrogated after raids on monkey labs. I lean closer toward her.

"I told you. I can't help."

She drops me flat on my feet and turns without a word. The thug handcuffs me and pulls me out of the door. I struggle, and he clamps a sweaty hand over my mouth before I can scream. Tobacco wafts into my nostrils. Where does he get ahold of that? Tobacco plants were wiped out in the Extinction.

The thug shoves me into the back seat of a long black car and shuts the door. "Where are you taking me?" I demand. Paloma is still in our house, while I'm in the car. This is extreme violation.

He ignores me, and I kick the back of the seat. "My fiancé works for Tremaine. You'll be sorry for this."

At that moment, she enters the car. "I report to him and the entire Hexagon board, so shut up and be grateful I didn't shoot you."

Now I'm scared. I glance out the window as the car pulls away, hoping someone will see me, but the streets are dark. Curfew is in place. My heart beats into my throat.

The car leaves the gates of the compound and drives onto a bumpy road. The handcuffs slam against my back repeatedly, and I can feel a bruise coming on. In the rearview mirror, I see the thug's eyes following me, as if I am ready to jump out and make my escape.

The black sky presses in on me. Out here they can do anything. Open the door and roll me out on the dusty ground for a wild dog to attack. Tie me up to a stake until I beg them to take me home. *I won't beg.*

Five minutes later, the car pulls into a grey concrete bunker hidden deep inside a valley. The thug jabs a gun into my back, directing me down a brightly lit corridor. I hear Paloma's heels heading in the other direction. *Make sure your watch stays with you,* Andrew had said.

I don't even know where I am.

10

THE THUG shoves me into a windowless room. There is one desk, three chairs, and one faded poster on the dingy walls. He pushes me toward the hard plastic chair with a loose back. Of course. They want to make me uncomfortable, make me fidget. I won't give them that satisfaction.

Paloma enters the room and circles the table. Once she's done stalking, she pulls a padded chair from underneath the white table so slowly that it echoes among the concrete walls. She leans on the back of the chair, tapping her red fingernails slowly, like a death march. I count the number of taps, think of a tune in my head; anything to keep me calm.

After seventy taps, she sits down, remains motionless, and stares at me. Our eyes lock, and I count the seconds. In the periphery, people walk past the door, stop and stare in, then move on. I don't shift my focus from her, and keep my body still in the seat. Although I know it won't happen, I keep hoping the third person will appear.

I look at her cold, beady eyes, her blanched face, and form a picture in my mind: she's a hoarder, lives with her mother, is afraid of rats. The image makes me smile inside and helps to alleviate the tension. I still don't know how security in the new Hexagon works. Is there even any justice? It is only corporate rule now, so that interrogation is a moot point. Still, I see it in her eyes: the joy of questioning, the power she feels. She was probably a beat cop in her time.

Paloma takes a drink of water, licks her lips with a look of satisfaction, and sets the glass back on the table. Inside, I'm shaking, but I fix my gaze on her and don't even drop my eyes to the water glass. My face is stealth.

Suddenly, she breaks the silence. "I feel like I'm back in high school detention," she says in a light voice. "Remember those days? I found them such a waste of time. Boring."

I'm used to these tactics: create a non-threatening atmosphere with casual conversation, claim to share beliefs, get your suspect to like you, to trust you because you're like them.

"I remember what my math teacher used to say." I continue to look straight at her the entire time I'm talking. I won't play her game. "An intelligent mind is never bored." She wants my eyes to move to the right, so she can determine how my brain activates memory. Then she will ask a basic question about Andrew's files to determine my deception.

One step ahead of you, bitch.

Paloma motions with her stubby fingers, and the lights dim. A holographic screen with my image on it pops up overhead.

"Larissa Kenders." She looks up at the screen. "A lot of charges for a seventeen-year-old."

I stare her down. I'm not talking.

"Classical music training since the age of three." She nods her head as she continues to read. "The standard. Kid gets everything she wants, then feels she has to rebel against her parents. You chose punk. Screaming lyrics. Violence."

Punk is always misunderstood, but now's not the time to get into it. I remain quiet. Motionless. Staring her down with razor eyes.

She shakes her head. "I can't understand why Andrew would be interested in you."

I got into university earlier than he did, bitch. "He has a dark side."

Paloma swipes at another folder. "Public mischief. Chaining yourself to a guard rail along a race track."

"It's a blood sport," I snap.

"Trespassing, forcible entry, vandalizing property. All to release two thousand minks and foxes."

I wrinkle my nose. "It was animal cruelty."

"Firebombing."

"It was a political protest." I straighten in my chair. "If you make peaceful revolution impossible, you make violent revolution inevitable." A quote from John F. Kennedy she's probably never heard.

"It's labelled here as terrorism. And," she punctuates each word, "this investigation has never been closed. We can keep it that way."

Don't try and blackmail me. I say nothing, but fold my shaking hands under the table where she can't see them.

She gets up, the chair legs scraping along the floor. "You think your fans will save you, Larissa?"

Do NOT address me by my first name.

She waves her hand into a fist, and the screen disappears. One bright light shines down on me. "You're a punk musician, not a chart-busting pop artist. Most people haven't even heard of your band, let alone your name. Your fans are primarily teens, most of them with their own charges. We could bust half of them for drugs right at your concerts. They'd switch their loyalties in a second."

You're wrong. You don't know punk. It's standing up for what we believe in. It's standing up against vermin like you. It's dropping you to the ground; it's squishing you between our toes like mud.

Then she gets up and leaves the room. Just like that, my wild imaginings stop.

She makes me wait. I try and count the minutes, but after half an hour it becomes tedious. I know one of the walls is a screen, and she's watching me every second. I rest my head on the table, close my eyes, and get comfortable. Nerves of steel. Keep up the facade.

When she enters the room again, she's holding a card. "A plain paper card. Digitally undetected, so keep it on you, Larissa."

My first name again? It's reserved for scumbags, like my father. Then again, she's in the same classification.

She lays it on the table, but I don't pick it up. "Let me spell it out for you clear and simple. Andrew has stolen from us."

Andrew doesn't steal. "You need his brain, then, because everything is stored there."

She jabs her finger at me. "Everything he does is owned by the company, not him. All his research. All his codes."

"Prove he stole something."

"We know what he was working on." She throws her hands up in the air. "We funded it." She leans over the table. "That's why we own it." She shoots her body up in the air, her blunt ends swinging in front of her face. "He had a breakthrough in VR technology, and we want it back."

I feel sweat beading underneath my bangs, and swallow hard. "I don't know what you're talking about."

She circles around behind me. "Ask lover boy." She bends in so close that I get a whiff of her perfume. Neroli. Haven't smelled that in years.

I feel her hot breath on my ear. "There are consequences if he sells it," she continues.

"There is no one else who could afford it," I state, but my words fall on deaf ears.

I now wonder what Andrew was alluding to the other night. What dark secret has he stumbled upon, that they're now hunting him down? Obviously they didn't find what they were looking for in our home. If they started with me, where will they go to next? He's in danger, and I have to find him.

She presses her hand hard into my shoulder. "If he returns what he's taken, we won't press charges."

Her words are hollow, and I remain resolutely quiet. Eventually she waves me off and motions to the thug, saying, "Get her out of here."

As I pass her by, her grey eyes pierce mine. "Contact me if you hear from him," she spits.

Like hell I will. I'll find him before you do.

11

THEY PULL the sheet over Andrew's face, and my body lurches forward with such convulsions that Corporal catches me before I keel over. I don't know how long I cry, but Corporal simply holds my body, repeating, "Shh, shh."

He's talking, but I can't take it in. Words drift in and out: "take care of you . . . there is life out there . . ." I look at the white sheet over Andrew's corpse, and all I can think of is one thing: Andrew is gone. He's literally gone, the very day after I talked with him in Nirvana, and then only for one brief minute when he told me he was in trouble. If only I had asked more, or gone back into Nirvana right then, but he told me to lay low, and I listened.

I glare at Paloma. While she had me cornered in the cement room, Andrew may have been reaching out again, unable to find me.

I can't shake the image of how he died from my mind. They say he was testing something in the mobile lab out in the desert, and there was an explosion.

Paloma walks up to me. "There will be an investigation into his death, of course. You'll need to stay here."

Our eyes collide. She's insinuating that I'm a suspect, just as she did in the bunker the other night, and it halts my grief. I consider my options. Protest with Corporal by my side. *Unfair.* Bolt for the door. *Nowhere to go.* Look her squarely in the eye as if I'm not phased in the least.

"I want to know everything you find out." My voice is hard and cold.

"That's confidential," she blurts. "You're not his wife, so we can't divulge it."

I narrow my eyes. "I'm his fiancée."

"Did he have a will?" Her eyes follow my every movement.

"No. He was twenty."

"Can't help you, then."

I look back at Corporal, and he sighs. "I checked with Tremaine. There's nothing I can do." Andrew told me to trust no one. Did he mean Corporal, as well?

I turn back to Paloma, my nostrils flaring. "What was he testing?" I ask.

"That's confidential also."

"He was a programmer, not a chemist. What could explode?" He had told me he was testing something, but he hadn't said what. And he hadn't said anything about taking the mobile lab. Usually he let me know if he'd be gone at length.

She shrugs. "We haven't determined that yet. A system could have short circuited. Something simple."

"Simple?" I bark. "There's nothing simple when someone has died." I keep thinking back to that short conversation we had in Nirvana. *Lay low,* he said. Was that the last communication he had with anyone?

"There will be a public announcement," Corporal says gently. "It won't take more than a day to determine the cause. More than likely it was an accident."

An accident. I heard that excuse years ago, when the leader of the animal rights group got too close to the truth about a university-corporate partnership. Either way, I want to find out what Andrew was working on, and what really happened to him. But, they'll be watching me like a hawk.

12

DR. GURMAN'S jowls sway as he leans back in his chair, the leather creaking under the weight of his body. "Everyone has a loss in their lives. That includes me. It's just a matter of how we deal with it."

I'm silent. I don't know if I trust him. He's old school, still holding a pen and paper. His only redeeming factor is that every thought isn't being recorded into Hexagon's system if he's writing them down.

"I lost my spouse a few years ago. I wasn't functional. Couldn't even work for a few months." He puts his pen down with a sincere smile. "In my line of work, we're very good at dishing out advice, but since this is my job, no one was here to offer me guidance. I don't want that happening to you."

The gentle words are a soothing balm, and I feel myself relax, if only for being understood.

"I just can't think about Andrew without that image of how he died," I admit. "The fire."

Gurman nods, his eyes warm and inviting. "Everyone has an image that haunts them. Or a memory they're trying to overcome."

"I can't shake the thought of him trapped in a room or under a toppled desk, knowing I was so close but could do nothing."

"We all feel the same way. We all loved Andrew." He looks down, then back up at me. "My wife and I had an argument before she left for work. She stormed out of our house and drove off. A head-on collision. Was she still caught up in anger, and not paying enough attention to the road? What if I had driven her, as I usually do?" He shrugs. "Probably none of it would have made a difference; it's hard to avoid a swerving transport truck. Maybe we'd both be dead."

I'm surprised at our similarities; at the way a Hexagon official is opening up to me. I just look at him, blinking back tears.

"All this is to say, Kenders, that I felt the same way when my wife died. It's easy for me to say this now, years later, but there's nothing you could have done."

"I know. That's what makes it worse."

"Why?"

"Because for all those times when he was there for me, for all those times that he helped me, I couldn't be there when he needed me." I don't have enough details on his death yet. I can't tell him about those few minutes in Nirvana, when Andrew warned me.

"That's your own guilt speaking."

I know that, but it doesn't make it easier. I feel the tears welling in the back of my head, and I press my teeth together. All I replay in my mind is that conversation before Paloma stormed into our home. Andrew was in trouble, and I did nothing. I should have gone to Terk. Or Corporal.

Gurman leans his chin on his folded hands. "We never know when that time will come. When our last moment will be."

I wipe away one solitary tear. If I had known it would be the last time, I wouldn't have fallen back asleep. I would have made love to him, and told him all the things I wanted to say.

As if reading my mind, Gurman asks, "If there was one thing you could say to Andrew, what would it be?"

"Don't go."

Gurman puts his pen down. "Why?"

"It's what I told him that morning. I just wanted him to stay."

"And he didn't?"

I bite my lip to fight back the tears. "He had lab work to do."

"What was he working on?"

"I'm not sure. He was working hard on something. He said . . ." I clench my fists. I know where this is going. He's trying to find out if I'm a prime suspect. Or if Andrew told me something. I'm not a stupid pod operator, Dr. Gurman. Not a raging punk musician. *Watch what you say, Kenders. Always be on guard with Hexagon. No one is your friend.* I look back at Dr. Gurman, grab a tissue, and dab at my eyes.

"It's hard for me to talk about Andrew."

I bury my head in my hands for a few moments to buy myself some time, in order to determine how I will orchestrate this situation. I look up at him. "Sorry. Andrew just didn't talk much about his work. He always said it was too complicated."

I watch Dr. Gurman make a notation in his notepad. Who writes anymore nowadays? Everything is electronic. Are these his own personal notes? Ones that can't get into the system?

Dr. Gurman places his pen squarely at the edge of the desk, and then folds his hands. "You're experiencing flashbacks. It's quite normal for what you're going through; it was a very traumatic experience. What's happening, though, is that you're not letting the natural process of grief start."

"This is grief. Whatever it is."

"Definitely," he says as he leans back in his chair. "You're a musician, Kenders."

I nod.

"And quite a good one. You had a stream of songs."

I nod, not sure where this is going.

"Which was your favourite?"

"'Rhetoric.'"

"What are the lyrics?"

"The chorus is:

Your curved lips disguise

Rhetoric

Your rehearsed lines are

Rhetoric

It's all bullshit lies

Rhetoric

Fuck off and die

Rhetoric."

Dr. Gurman takes a deep breath. "So, what's the song about?"

"A monkey that was tested in a university lab. Holes were drilled into its skull, metal restraint devices screwed into its head, and electrodes inserted into its brain. It was then immobilized in restraint chairs with its head bolted into place as its brain activity was recorded doing behavioural tasks. The head of the department gave us rhetoric to get rid of us."

"So, what did you do?"

"We staged a sit-in with our fans outside of the lab, invited the media, and screamed the chorus at the top of our lungs until the monkey was released. It was one of our most successful campaigns."

"I recall that in the news. There's a real story arc to that song. That chorus is only one part. Each verse tells the story of what happened."

"Yes." *Where is this going?*

"In the same way, your focus on that last moment of Andrew's life is only allowing one part of him to exist in your memory. There's only one part of your life together that exists for you. But there's so much more, isn't there?"

I just nod. I want him to help me, but I don't know if I can trust him.

"You see, Kenders, you're focusing on the way Andrew died, but that's not his life. I want to help you detraumatize that memory, and recall other moments, so you can feel free to grieve properly." He waits for a few seconds, and then continues. "Will you let me?"

"What will you do?"

"My prescription is an overnight in Nirvana. Go back to the experiences you had with Andrew. Or visit some of the places where you were together before the Extinction happened. Reconnect with that part of your life."

I'm not sure what to say. Andrew and I never did an overnight in Nirvana. I don't even know if I'm ready to see Andrew for that long now that he's dead. I'm quite comfortable missing Andrew right now.

I look up at Dr. Gurman. "I don't want to get over Andrew."

"It doesn't work that way," he says in a gentle voice. "I just want to stop the image of how he died from being front and centre in your life. I want you to feel at peace."

I can't imagine peace right now, not ever, if Andrew isn't in my life. Right now, I can't even sit by a candle without thinking of the fire.

What I mostly don't want is Hexagon listening in to every thing I might say while in Nirvana. I know they monitor everything. When Andrew briefly appeared for a few seconds during that training session with Corporal, I know he was working on developing some form of communication that could be executed without being spotted. But Andrew won't be there to scramble signals this time, and I know Hexagon will be watching.

13

NIRVANA

Silver Moon

I AM in the field, the silver moon rising, the grasses scratching the edges of my legs, the crickets calling all around me. Under Dr. Gurman's prescription, I could choose from pre-set destinations, or select saved experiences. I came back to the apple orchard where Andrew and I last went.

Everywhere I look, there's colour: a canopy of deep green leaves, the meadow dotted with yellow sunflowers and purple alfalfa, butterflies sipping nectar from a cluster of yarrow. I pluck off a clover blossom and chew on a petal, then reach for a dandelion and hold it to my chin. It's a world I had known once, before the Extinction, and to see flowers that once were so commonplace fills me with an unexpected joy. I've grown accustomed to our new dreary world—the muted tones of sandstone and dust swirling in the air—but this is the world I want.

I close my eyes and imagine the world as it once was, but really, I'm waiting for Andrew. Time seems to pass slower with one's eyes closed. Bizarre, but it's true. Mom always told me that watching a boiling pot caused it to take longer. Could she have been right about so many things? The thought alone pops my eyes open, till I shake off the notion. I rest my head back down onto the soft grass and press my lids shut, waiting for Andrew to appear.

The longer it takes, the more I wonder whether or not this experience is healthy for me. Is Gurman suggesting this prescription for my benefit, or is it what Hexagon wants? Then, do I have a choice?

Still, I'm plagued by the thought. Seeing Andrew again, even if it's virtual, will make the inevitable parting all the more difficult. I could be grieving all over again, every time.

I hear footsteps, and open my eyes to Andrew's freckled face and warm smile. He's carrying a carved walking stick with his initials whittled into the edge. A.M. "I made it for you," he says, and tosses it toward me.

There's a natural indentation in the hooked handle for my thumb, and I hold on to it in a daze while he runs toward me, picks me up, and swings me around.

I wrap my arms around his broad shoulders. "It's you. You're alive." I run my palms along his sinewy back and arms, then grasp on to his steady hands and just look at him: his short cropped hair, crooked teeth, dimpled chin.

"I knew you were. I knew it." I hold him, running my hands over his body again and again, and then the tears flow. "I'm sorry," I sob, "I just don't want to let you go again."

"I know," he says soothingly, his brown eyes soft. "I know."

"Who are you? What are you? I mean, I was plugged in just like I do to people. I know where I am. Nirvana. It's not real, it's programmed, but I need you to be real. To feel you're alive somewhere. That in some way, I can reach you."

I can't hold back the tears. I'm struck by the familiarity of him. Everything is so real. Every detail in his face, the timbre of his voice, the twinkle in his eyes. While I know it isn't him, I succumb to what my heart wants. I kiss him, gathering his shirt in my fingers, groping for more of him.

As our tongues explore, as my hands trail down his sinewy back, I start to cry again. "I miss you." I wipe my tears on his shirt sleeve. "Chopper sits on your slippers. He's waiting for you to come back." My breaths are short and quick. "I want you to stay."

"I wish I could."

"What's it like?"

"What?"

"Being gone . . . Not seeing me anymore." I can't say it. Can't say the word "death." Can't form my lips around that word without my throat closing up.

"It's all new to me," Andrew replies. "I'm lost right now. Seeing you, it's my only constant."

"You know I'll always love you."

"I know."

"There's always a home here for you. Always."

We hold each other for a long time, and are silent again.

"Andrew . . . where do you go?"

His face is blank. And then I realize what I'm doing. I'm so caught up in needing to see him, in wanting to believe he's still here, that I've fallen for the very thing Nirvana represents: the virtual, not the real. This isn't Andrew.

"You okay?" he asks.

I shake my head. "No, because you're not real."

"I picked you this apple." He hands it to me.

I toss it away. "I want a mango, not an apple."

"I'm not magic, you know."

"I'm making a point," I say, matter-of-factly. "It wasn't programmed in, or it would be here."

"Did you program me?"

"No, but you're probably part of this experience," I snap. "I'm sure Corporal had you coded into this system. Gurman is monitoring every word I say."

He pulls the carved stick from his side. "And this? It's not programmed."

He hands it to me, and I throw it back at him. "It's not real, anyhow. Nothing is. Not even you."

"Trust me, Kenders." His voice wavers, and his face twists in agony. "It can't be any other way right now."

I can't say why, but I believe him. And yet, I'm angry. Did Andrew know he was going to die when he left? Did he program all these words, all these images of himself, so he would always be near? I kick at the ground, and jump up and away. I'm not angry with him. It's the computer I hate, and the system that created Nirvana; the system that killed him. This isn't Andrew; it's a holograph, an electronic manipulation. He couldn't still be alive, could he?

"Is it you? Is it really you?" What if he uploaded his brain? Then this would be him, in a sense.

He laughs. "Of course it is."

"I mean like last time?"

"The same."

Do I need to be cryptic if he's dead? I'm not sure. I'm not sure about anything.

"But the last time I saw you, were you dead then?"

"Dead?" Andrew's eyes open wide. "I'm not dead. I'm here."

"But the fire. You were barely recognizable. Your face . . ." The thought of it makes me cry, and he holds me.

"Kenders," Andrew says softly. "I'm here."

"Then come back to me," I wail.

"I can't right now. I promise you, if I could, I would."

I bury my face in my hands. I'm not sure what to believe anymore. What is real and what isn't?

"Kenders?"

His voice interrupts my thoughts.

"Yeah."

He pushes my bangs from my forehead and looks deep into my eyes. "Let's forget about everything else but right now." I feel his breath on my neck as he lowers his lips onto my earlobe. "This isn't a dream. It's real." He kisses the back of my neck, my shoulders; runs his tongue along my collarbone. I moan as I lie back into the grasses.

"Don't ever leave me," I beg.

"I'm always with you," he whispers.

Our fingers entwine and he lowers his body onto mine, just as I feel a growing pressure on my head–the familiar sign that my time is up. Tears fill my eyes, and after a few moments, I'm pulled away from Andrew, away from Nirvana, and back to reality under the weight of my headset.

14

I'M ALWAYS with you. Those words keep returning to me during the bumpy ride home, and I close my eyes, pretending that I'm still back in the fields, his body inside of mine. I clench my fists against the memory, trying to shake it from my being. It's a dream. It's not real. It's virtual reality.

I work there. I remove people's headsets every day and see their confusion, their in-between state. Now I'm at the same point.

Without opening my eyes, I touch the cold moulded plastic of the seat. I tap it with my fingernail and hear that tinny sound. This is Earth I'm on. This is the physical reality. But, would it be any different in Nirvana? Andrew has perfected it to such a level that every sight and sound is as authentic as in real life.

I reach my hands to my head. No headset, just the stringy strands of my hair, greasy from days of not washing it, not caring about anything but my own loss.

"Kenders!"

I open my eyes as the bus door unlatches. It's back to reality: a night in our empty bunker. A long, sleepless night with Chopper curled up in bed next to my feet rather than Andrew's warm body spooning mine.

As I step out of the bus, the driver hands me a package. "Corporal asked me to give you this."

I walk toward the main door and stop in my tracks. Leaning against the handle is a walking stick. I turn it over in my hand and see the carved initials: A.M. I slide my thumb into the hooked handle; the natural indentation is there.

I run my fingers over the carving again and again, opening my eyes to the stark air, touching the metal door, and then the stick. *He is alive. He is here.*

I look around, but see no one. I hold the stick in my hand and walk faster down the long hallway that leads to our home. I open the door and sink to the floor, running my fingers along my mouth where Andrew had kissed me hours before. Were those two hours real?

Chopper's cold, wet nose pushes against my hand, and the paper bag rustles. I have completely forgotten about it, and I unroll the top of the bag. A hand-written note sits inside and reads: "You asked me for it." Underneath is a mango.

15

I MARCH into Corporal's office. "Tell me where he is," I bark.

"What are you talking about?"

"I saw him."

"Of course you did, but Nirvana isn't real, Kenders."

"He's real to me. He's alive."

"It's supposed to be realistic. That's what virtual reality is." Corporal starts pacing as he explains. "It's a pastime. A game. Leisure entertainment. It's anything but real."

"I saw him."

Corporal places his hands on my shoulders and says so convincingly, "He's dead, Kenders," that I almost doubt what I have seen.

I slam the note on his desk. "It's his handwriting."

He looks at me, the slant of his eye telling me to be quiet. "Kenders," he says in a soothing voice, "we've been through this. Andrew is dead."

I snatch the note back and clutch it to my chest. In the time it takes for Corporal to get up to shut the door, pour me some coffee, and sit back down, I play through the entire evening.

I had cradled the engraved stick and gone straight to my bunker, pulled out the heart-shaped box that Andrew had given me, and opened one of the cards. It was in the same loopy scrawl of his. *You asked me for it.* I knew it was his writing, but I had begun to doubt everything, and compared the note next to each card he had given me. *He was alive.*

I had slept with the stick that night, curled over it like a doll, summoning Andrew to come back to me, begging to at least see him in a dream. This morning, I hid it underneath my mattress.

Corporal hands me a cup of water and taps my hand lightly underneath. I look up at him as his eyes motion to the far right. I don't look right away; I know better than that. Corporal and I had developed this code during VR training, and I know he will lead me to an answer or clue in a natural way eventually.

He walks toward the bookshelf, pulls out a holo-file, and places it on top of the shelf. My eyes follow his hand, and then I automatically glance upward, straight into a small camera tucked in a corner. Immediately I look toward him.

"Don't pull out the file."

"It's all I can do. Show you what we've done to investigate the accident."

"It wasn't enough."

"Have you been to see Dr. Gurman?"

I fold my hands, confused by what is happening, but following Corporal's lead. I have learned enough about the new surveillance system from Terk. While he explained the cost of monitoring every microscopic camera hidden inside each home and public space, he mostly lamented about the lack of Hexagon funding for research. Despite the assurances that funding would increase, Terk had never seen it, and if Andrew hadn't insisted on keeping the library open for his research, all of the books might have been lost. Theirs was one of the few libraries that hadn't been digitized. Yet.

Corporal is now beside me, his hand on my shoulder. "Let's go for a walk. The fresh air will do you some good."

I nod, and follow him outside. The long walk down the hallway, the echo of our shoes against the concrete tiles, all make me feel more alone and empty.

"I know this is a difficult time," Corporal says. "And I'm here for you. Let's walk and talk."

I just nod again. I have no idea where this is going, no idea what's happening, and my brain is trying to get caught up with the events of the last few hours.

"Tell me what you're feeling."

"Confused."

He opens the door for me. "What can we do to give you comfort?"

I squint at the bright light and shrug. If only I knew what I was feeling. Everyone reminds me that Andrew is dead, but now there's a part of me that feels he's alive.

We cross the threshold of the parking lot, open the gate, and walk across the road toward the park. He taps my shoulder twice as he motions for me to go in front of him. I know that code, and stay quiet.

We walk through the forest trail, the only area where birds sing and trees grow; artificial trees, engineered to look like the real thing, and birds that are wired to fly and sing via loudspeakers. They are all well hidden, though, and if I leave my skeptical eyes behind for just a moment, I can forget where I am. This woodland used to be a haven for me, but now, given Corporal's code, I know it's also under watchful eyes. There are probably cameras in every branch and microphones in each bird that swoops over our heads. I stay silent.

When we exit the trail and walk through the gate, Corporal waves off the car that comes to pick him up. Anything beyond this point is considered to be dangerous. Apparently feral animals and desperate survivors are the biggest threat, although I don't see how anyone could subsist out here.

Corporal reaches into the guard room for a pistol and pack. "We're walking today, boys. Just a little stroll into the valley. It's clear today?"

"Yes, sir," the guard confirms.

"At ease."

We cross into the open landscape, and an emptiness fills my body. Ahead are stark limestone cliffs and barren hills that carry an eerie air.

To the right and left are sand dunes; former woodlands and lakes that once glowed in the setting sun. Andrew had shown me archival photos of the area from when it was a national park with campgrounds that circled the lakes. Now it's all desolate, and the air is thick with dust that coats my clothes and hands. Each time I breathe in, I feel a pasty film in my mouth.

Corporal steps into a rocky passage that narrows between two steep walls farther down the pathway. As we descend, he speaks in a lowered tone.

"We only have a minute before the signal is picked up at the top of the ridge, so I'll be quick. You have to trust me. Don't say anything about the mango."

"Is he alive?"

"I can't tell you."

"Don't play with me."

"I'm not."

"Are you spying on Nirvana?"

"No."

"Can you see everything that happens there? Is it some virtual reality game for Hexagon? Do you sit around and laugh in your private chamber at your pathetic . . ."

Corporal grabs my shoulder. We are approaching the hill.

"Listen to me," he says in the same calm, soothing voice. "I'm glad you trust us. See, you just need to talk about this more. Get it off your chest. And if counselling isn't for you, and you need to talk with me, I'm always available."

"Thank you."

"And I agree with you. This desolate country is soothing for the soul. Like the arctic. Nothing but yourself and your thoughts. I will bring you out here regularly. I owe that to Andrew."

My heart sinks, and all I can do is nod. We walk in silence, engulfed by the rock formations and the swirls of sand that gather at our feet. I think back to the last time I had been in the desert with Andrew. We had driven far into the valley, miles from the last guarded entry point, and made love in the shade of the truck. Andrew had chosen the spot because it was out of camera range, out of earshot of those who monitored every move that was made. Andrew told me then, with his hands clasped around mine, that if something were ever to happen to him, Corporal would take care of me. I would need to trust him.

But how can I trust Corporal when I think Andrew's alive, and he's telling me he's dead? And how does he know about the mango, and what does it mean? I see the rocky passage that narrows between two steep walls, and kick up sand as I walk faster toward the ridge.

The moment we descend, I ask, "Can I talk freely?"

He nods as he removes a black case from the pack. He stops to hide it in a cavity behind a rockface before continuing.

"What's that?" I ask.

"There isn't time to explain now. I'll tell you later."

"What about the stick?" I push.

"What stick?"

"Don't play with me, Corporal."

"I'm not."

We crest the hill, and for the first time, I realize this is even beyond Corporal.

16

NIRVANA

The Code

I'M IN the apple orchard again, the silver moon rising, the grasses scratching the edges of my legs, the crickets calling all around me; every detail as it was last time. Andrew walks up to me with the same carved walking stick. "I made it for you," he says, and tosses it toward me.

I let it drop, wondering if that will throw off the algorithm, but the program just churns along. He runs toward me, picks me up, and swings me around. My heart sinks.

We go through the motions: my same questions, his same answers. He asks me the same questions, as well, and I respond. What can I say? I want this, even though I know it's not real. Everything about Andrew is acute and strong: his slow-forming smile, his athletic build, his sharp analytical mind. Even if this is his virtual self.

"You okay?" he asks.

I shake my head. "No, because you're not real."

"I picked you this apple." He hands it to me.

I sigh. I might as well have some fun with this one.

"I want a peach, not an apple."

"Trust me, Kenders." His voice wavers, and his face twists in agony. "It can't be any other way."

He's skipped a whole series of lines. Is it because I changed one word, from mango to peach, or is it because Andrew *was* with me in Nirvana last time?

I bury my face in my hands. I'm exhausted and confused.

"Kenders?"

His voice interrupts my thoughts.

"Yeah."

He pushes my bangs from my forehead, and looks deeply into my eyes. My heart sinks again. Every action is repeating itself from the last time. Nothing has changed. I can't take it anymore.

Then, just as I'm about to get up and run away, he says, "Remember where we made love the first time?"

I don't think he asked this question last time, but my mind has been so muddled lately.

"Of course."

I will never forget that day. It was after our graduation, and Hexagon was enticing him to join their team. They brought Andrew to the Bubble for a conference, and we arrived a day early.

"Go back there. It will comfort you." Andrew takes my hands. "Then come back here, and we'll reminisce about it. You can tell me over coffee."

He winks at me, but my breath has stopped. *You can tell me over coffee.* This is not a loop. Andrew never winks. And he never used our code when we were together in Nirvana. I know this for a fact. There was no need.

Until now.

"Let's forget about everything else but right now," he says. I feel his breath on my neck as he lowers his lips onto my ear lobe. "This isn't a dream. It's real." He kisses the back of my neck, my shoulders; runs his tongue along my collarbone.

It's like we're suddenly back in the loop of the experience I had last time. Word for word. Action for action. It's no use changing anything; he will respond as the virtual Andrew always does.

"I'm always with you," he whispers as we lie back into the grasses.

He reaches for my fingers, and as he lowers his body onto mine, I feel a growing pressure on my head. That same familiar sign that I'm returning to Earth; floating back into my physical reality under the weight of my headset.

This time, though, my eyes don't fill with tears as I'm pulled away from Andrew. I have too much work to do. Even if Andrew pre-recorded these conversations before he died, he's telling me where to go to find answers. I have to get to the Bubble like he said, and figure this out.

17

I'M CERTAIN Andrew is alive now, and I have to get the information he needs. I figure it's his research. That must be what Paloma was digging for in his desk at our place, and I want to get to it before she does. Maybe Andrew will tell me more next time I talk to him in Nirvana. Or maybe he'll be there in that room in the Bubble, where we made love for the first time.

What I need to do is act as though I still believe Andrew is dead, and pretend that I'm distraught and confused; it will keep Paloma off of my trail. I also have to find a reason for them to send me to the Bubble.

I start with Corporal over lunch, and ask to look through the holo-file on Andrew's death.

He nods, but still asks, "Why?"

I shrug. "Closure, I guess." I look down at my feet, then back up at him. "It's the last traces of him."

What I really want is to find out why Andrew died. He needed my help, so obviously the information must somehow be available to me.

The folder itself is a representation of everything that is wrong with Hexagon. Once the file is closed, the paper will become digitized. It's all Hexagon did for years in the Barracks, until they made it impossible to retrieve archival resources, and removed access to any paper files or books.

There's one paper folder left. I open it, and lift up the first page: a picture of Andrew. Young, confident, full of ambition; just the way he was when I met him. He had received the university's biggest scholarship award, funded by Hexagon. People would approach him in the streets, asking to join his team, and I would snicker in the background, knowing he was uncomfortable with all the attention.

I press my finger to the photo and run it along his long jaw, touching each freckle. A tear trickles down my cheek, and I wipe it with my shirt sleeve.

Corporal hands me a tissue box. "You okay?" he asks.

I nod.

"You can look through this tomorrow."

I shake my head. "I'm fine," I insist.

It's a lie, but it feels like everything is suddenly different. I have a sense that many things will change, and I will never see this file again. If there is anywhere that I might find a clue, it will be in these documents.

I turn the photo over in my hands, and see a code with writing and someone's signature on the back. These numbers might give me access to some hidden files, some clue as to why Andrew was in trouble before he died. Or, they could reveal what Hexagon is hiding. I flip the photo back to Andrew's face and place the folder into my lap, rifling through the rest of the pages. There are two stacks of paper stapled together, and another set of photos.

I fake sobbing and let the contents of the folder slide from my lap, directing them under Corporal's desk, out of view of the camera. I plunge toward it, quickly tucking Andrew's photo up my sleeve as I gather the papers.

Corporal is beside me, picking up some of the photos.

"You should do this tomorrow. It's too much," he urges.

All I have so far are the numbers on the back of Andrew's photo. I need more.

"No, no. It's fine," I insist, lifting up the next page. I run my eyes over every word on the waiver Andrew had signed for the research program, scrutinizing each sentence, looking for something I might have missed before. I try to look beyond the legal jargon I don't understand to see if there's anything unusual.

I read one paragraph again and again, trying to commit it to memory, resting my arm against the tabletop to keep the photo from slipping into view:

> *I acknowledge that my Research position with HEXAGON carries with it the potential for death, serious injury, or permanent dispersal and disappearance during the study of Earth, celestial bodies, or cyberspace. The risks include, but are not limited to: actions of other people including, but not limited to, participants, volunteers, spectators, coaches, research officials, research monitors, and/or funders of the research; lack of physical resources; inclement weather; and/or other natural or unnatural cyber conditions. I hereby assume all of the risks of acting in this Research role and participating in this position.*

At the time, I hadn't asked Andrew enough about his work with Hexagon. It was yet another corporate-funded program for his graduate studies, and I was concentrating on my music.

He had told me once, "If anything ever happens to me, go to our special spot at U of T. I've put everything there."

I had raised a hand to my mouth in shock. "It still exists?"

"The gardens are bare, the trees are gone, but the buildings are still there. The bench. The rocks and walkway."

"Can we go?"

"It's too dangerous." He had looked away for a moment, then squeezed my hands tightly. "If anything happens, Corporal can take you."

I run my finger along the next page, and keep circling back to one line:

I acknowledge that this Accident Waiver and Release of Liability
(AWRL) form will be used by HEXAGON, and the sponsors of the
research in which I participate, and it will govern my actions and
responsibilities throughout my position.

A tear drops from my eye and onto the paper. Corporal hands me a
tissue. "You can continue tomorrow."

I turn to Corporal. "I want to go back to the university."

"Why?"

"Walk the grounds." I sigh. "A sense of closure. It was such a major
part of my life; it still feels fresh and real to me."

"It's so far away."

"Couldn't I go during a routine fly-over?"

Corporal shakes his head. "It's too dangerous."

"Andrew said you could take me anywhere."

"Things have changed, Kenders. I'm sorry."

I know better than to ask what has changed. I turn to the clause that
is the hardest for me to read:

In consideration of my application and permitting me to participate
in this research, I hereby take action for myself and my executors, ad-
ministrators, heirs, next of kin, successors, and assigns as follows: (A)
Waive, release, and discharge from any and all liability for my death,
disability, personal injury, property damage, property theft, or actions
of any kind that may hereafter accrue to me or my travelling during
my research, the following entities or persons: HEXAGON, and their
directors, officers, employees, volunteers, representatives, and agents,
the research sponsors, and research volunteers (B) Indemnify and hold
harmless all entities or persons mentioned in this paragraph from any
and all liabilities or claims made by other individuals or entities as a
result of my actions during this research.

I close my eyes and place down the folder.

I'm always with you. What did he mean?

I look up from the file. "I wish I could just talk with him one more time."

"That's always what we want," Corporal says in a gentle voice. "But you know what he feels. He loves you, Kenders."

His eyes meet mine, waiting for some kind of confirmation, but my heart has stopped cold. It's the only time he has spoken of Andrew in present tense, as if Andrew is still alive.

18

CORPORAL DOESN'T know everything, which means it goes higher than him, straight to Tremaine. Before I leave for the Bubble, I have to find out what I can here at Hexagon.

With that conviction, and the most destitute look I can manage spread over my face, I walk into Corporal's office. He's in a meeting with a few other people, but they leave the moment I enter, except for Paloma.

I glare at her. "I want her out of this room," I state flatly.

She looks at Corporal and he motions her to the door, saying firmly, "We'll talk after."

She shoves her chair back, her heels clicking on the ground, and knocks against me on her way out. In my mind, I stick my leg back and grab her arm, twisting her onto the floor in one fast move. I'm on top of her, my fist pounding her face, my elbow slamming her head, blood spurting from her mouth. But instead I stand there as a victim, quiet and sullen.

I'm the one playing you, bitch.

Corporal comes to my side. "How are you?"

I bite my lip back and pull out a tissue from my pocket, then bury my face in it. *Cry, dammit. Now!* I find it so hard to force tears when

I'm angry at everyone. Bitter with Hexagon, whom we trusted for all of these years.

Come on, Kenders. This is your acting debut. I think of myself back at the morgue, when I really believed Andrew was dead. I remember my short breathing, so I start there. I take in quick gasps, and then I let my shoulders heave. I imagine my life without him, and then, from deep within, I find the tears.

I look up at Corporal, and he's convinced.

"Sit down," he says.

I shake my head. "I'm sitting all the time. Sitting, talking to Gurman. Sitting in my bed, crying. I just need to get away."

"What do you mean?"

"Away from here. From memories. It's too much."

"What do you need?"

"Oh, just to get away from these walls. This compound."

"How about a walk?"

I let a look of hope cross my face.

"That one we took," Corporal suggests.

My shoulders drop, and I sigh. "I hadn't thought of that. It would be good."

"We can go now."

"I need to be alone." I conjure a look of distress. "I'm getting stressed with people around me."

"I won't say a word. I'll just be there for your safety."

I take a deep breath in. "Then I won't go. Nothing against you, I just can't . . ."

"I understand."

I plaster a look of despair on my face again. "Maybe I'll just walk in circles in the parking lot."

"No, no. That's not what you need." He leans against his desk. "Listen, just a short walk, okay?"

I nod, allowing a bit of hope to trickle into my face again. "Out where we walked . . . I could just go to the top of the ridge and back."

He nods in agreement. "You're in view most of the time that way."

"Thanks." I let a slight smile cross my face. "It's what I need. You always know me so well."

ONCE OUTSIDE, as we cross the threshold of the parking lot and walk toward the park, I plant my first seed regarding the Bubble.

"I wonder if I should get away for a while," I muse. "Maybe to the Bubble. I remember our last time there. We had this penthouse suite. I'd feel close to him there."

Corporal just nods, but doesn't bite, saying he'll put in a request for me like I want him to. I sense something else is on his mind. *What now?* Getting into the Bubble is like being sent on vacation. While I can file for a bereavement leave from work duties, there isn't always availability for non-residents at the Bubble.

I realize how risky this scheme is. Am I sure that Andrew is alive? I did see a charred corpse in the morgue. While there wasn't much of a body left, it did have similar facial features. But I didn't insist on seeing dental records or anything.

At the gated entrance, Corporal asks, "Clear today?"

"One feral, but in the distance," the guard confirms.

Corporal waves off the car. "Kenders is walking on her own today, boys. Just up to the first ridge. Keep your eyes peeled, though. If there's any trouble, get out there in a flash. We want her safe."

For a moment, I wonder if I've fallen into my own trap. Do they want me out here, without protection, to say it was another accident?

Corporal turns to me, shaking his finger as if I were a little kid. "No farther than the first ridge," he warns.

"I can go into the valley?"

He shakes his head, and my stomach drops.

"I like it in there. It's so peaceful," I beg.

Corporal draws a long breath and hesitates.

"I can take a gun."

He reaches into the pack and hands me one, looking at the guards, and then back at me.

"Be careful," is all he says.

When I step beyond the protected barricade, I get nervous. *Careful.* What was that look Corporal gave the guards?

I cross into the open landscape, looking back several times to ensure that no one is following me. I walk slowly; a calculated measure, so that I will have more time when I descend into the rocky passage.

Where before I saw an empty, stark landscape, now I see purpose. Could Andrew be hiding out here somewhere, watching me this very minute?

When I step into the rocky passage, I run between the two steep walls, straight to the cavity behind the rockface where Corporal hid the black case.

As I remove the case and see the combination lock, my heart sinks. I didn't think about that, and Lexie is the lock expert, not me. I bash the box against the rock, but nothing opens it. When I hear the echo within the narrow rockface, I stop. All I need is a bunch of people clambering down on me.

What code could it be?

I look at my watch. I have limited time before I need to appear on the other side of the ridge. I've calculated an extra minute because I'd walk more carefully through the passage, but I don't have more time than that. The last thing I want is someone following me. I try Corporal's birthday, and then his phone number. I even try the code that I found on the back of Andrew's photo.

Nothing works.

I'm running out of time. I dash up to the other side of the ridge, taking one slow step onto the top to make it seem like I took my time. I turn around to see the two guards still standing there. For a few minutes, I feign admiration of the view, all the while trying to think of other number sequences that would have some significance.

Then it dawns on me. I descend slowly, and after a few steps, run back toward the box. I enter the date of my father's accident.

The box opens.

I quickly rifle through the contents: photos and papers. I empty everything into my backpack, then dash up the hill and continue a slow walk back to the gate.

There's one thing I saw among the photos that alarms me, and I know just who to reach out to in the Bubble for help.

19

I CALL Lexie. She arrives with three suitcases and an entourage, but it's part of the plan. Tremaine is sure to notice a gorgeous blonde with as many cronies as he has, but he already had his eye on her in his Nirvana escapades. Her arrival is not only the hot topic of conversation at Hexagon for the week, but she has also agreed to speak with Tremaine backstage after the concert.

Sure enough, he's waiting backstage when the last number is up. Lexie has been playing him the entire time, raising her drumsticks enough to give him a good view of her bust, and riding up on the stool more than usual. Lexie knows how to put on a show. After her staid jazz performances, I know she was thrilled to let it loose again.

I watch Tremaine as he eyes Lexie, who is preparing to sign autographs with the fans and take photos with them. If Tremaine were a dog, he'd be drooling with his tongue on the floor. Pathetic man.

Finally, Lexie walks over to him.

"Where's your office?" She bats her long eyelashes.

"In the tower." Tremaine points to it from the window.

Lexie leans in for effect, brushing her breasts against his shoulder. "Are you on the top floor?"

He nods.

"I like guys that are on top."

He beams.

"Take me there. All of us girls."

"I like a threesome," he says with a sick grin.

Lexie and I step forward and giggle, and he holds out an arm for each of us. He doesn't recognize me behind my wig and heavy makeup. *Idiot.*

Within minutes his thugs disperse the crowd of fans, and we follow Tremaine into his car. Smooth black leather, hand-stitched and freshly polished. I'm not into cars, but I know one thing: it's not the same ride that we get in the Hexagon buses.

Lexie slides into the seat as if she were coming down on top of Tremaine. She knows what to do to hold his attention while I stand up and look out the rooftop window, then slip a wireless video camera into a slim opening in the roof.

The ride to his office is mercifully short, although when I step out, Tremaine reclines the seat with an open invitation for Lexie. What a loser.

As sickening as the ride was, I'm more aghast to be inside his office. While he waves off his thugs, we take a look around. You could fit two dozen bunkers into here. Next to his office he has an entire condo with a kitchen and living room, and of course, a bedroom. I'm sure he brings all the women up here.

Lexie asks him for details about the decor and particular art pieces, all the while scouting out where his secret hiding spots might be. When Tremaine refuses to take down a Picasso to prove it's real, Lexie reaches for the frame with her pouty lips and bared breasts. Anger flashes in Tremaine's eyes, and he immediately grabs her wrists, then catches himself. Busted! Lexie pours him a drink and leads him into the bedroom for the tour.

Two minutes later, she's back. "He's out," Lexie says, and hands me a pair of rubber gloves. We lift the Picasso off the wall, then Lexie holds a device to the lock mechanism and starts turning the dial. We're back in the activism days until she opens the lock and a second safe appears with a simple keyhole. I gasp, but Lexie smiles and holds up a key.

"That's what you were looking for in his pants?" I joke, and we both laugh.

We fall back into our old protocol. She opens the safe and goes through the files within, being careful not to disturb the placement of anything, as I scan the contents.

I pick up a holo-album and we click it open. Inside are photos of Tremaine with women; two, three, four or more, tied up or chained with whip marks. It's like they're animals in a lab experiment. We shut it off, click on a holo-cabinet, and open a folder labelled "Extinction."

The first screen is an overview with an Extinction timeline. It's the usual points that the media covered over the last ten years. First bee population declined, then commercial beekeeper operations failed. Then, without beekeepers, farmers couldn't attract enough wild bees to pollinate their fields, and their harvests failed as well.

The next screens track every product. Kale. Spinach. Avocados. Cucumbers. Tomatoes. What stands out to me is a profit column with staggering amounts. It all makes sense when I unfold a large flowchart.

"Look at this." My finger trails the first arrow, labelled "Control Food Production." There was a series of attempted solutions, such as GMO seeds, that involved steps of buying out smaller farms by raising the price of seeds till they weren't profitable. Eventually, the Food Production Control campaign was cancelled due to a high cost factor and deaths from the bacterial toxins and insecticides the plants produced.

I look at Lexie, and we both shake our heads in disbelief.

My finger follows the arrow to the next box, labelled "Produce Decline." This trail leads to a decision diamond with the text: "Less than 1/6 of almond production remains." I shake inside as I read the label in the next box: "Save the Bees Campaign."

What follows is a series of steps: "Hire a public relations firm to do a full-scale campaign about bees starved of the nutrition they need to help produce food for humans." My knees feel weak, and I sink into a nearby chair.

"We were a part of this," I mumble, and Lexie is instantly at my side. My hands are shaking as I stutter. "Remember that benefit concert we did for the bees?"

"The cross-country tour?" Lexie asks.

"We were pawns." I point to the name of the public relations company on the flowchart, the one that hired us, then to the next box.

"Hexagon funds research that proves bees are becoming undernourished," I read. I can't even speak the words in the next box, but I tap on it:

"Engineer plant with a chemical to decimate the bee population."

"Bastards!" Lexie shrieks as she reads the next box:

"Distribute plants free at events and to signees of online petition."

I clench my fists. "We handed out thousands of those packets at our concerts."

Lexie takes a deep breath, and when she speaks, her voice is sullen. "We threw them into the crowds by the buckets."

"I planted them in my own garden."

We skim over the rest of the info. We know that history. The low almond production led to less almond hulls and shells, which minimized animal feed. That created a decrease in nutrients for livestock, and ultimately, less dairy products. The loss of honey production eventually toppled the cosmetics industry, and the lack of cottonseed created a shortage of clothing, towels, and linens. Then we lost beef and dairy cows. The arrow finally leads to a red oval at the end of the page that simply reads: "Bee Extinction."

"We'll bring him down." I slam my fist on the table.

"Not a chance," Corporal's voice booms as the door opens.

20

CORPORAL GRABS Lexie's hands to handcuff her, and I bark, "Hive." Out of everything I saw in his briefcase, this one word seems to be a link.

He drops Lexie's hands and takes a swing at me. I duck and yell, "Touch me, and that goes public, Corporal."

"You don't have a leg to stand on."

"I have your entire black case, so back off."

Corporal steps aside. "You're fighting the wrong person."

"You're one of them."

"I protected you, and . . ."

"Spare me." I push him aside. "You were in on this all along."

"It's not what you think. I'm . . ."

"Guilty." I slide the door shut. "Who knows you're here?"

"Only me."

"I don't believe you."

"I'm head of security. I get the first camera alert." He speaks into his watch. "Terk, all is fine. Erase all footage from the last fifteen minutes. Don't wake Paloma."

Corporal glares at me. "What did you do to him?" he demands.

"He's drugged," Lexie snaps. "He's got another half hour."

Corporal turns to me. "Get your ass out of here." He points to Lexie. "Be here when he wakes up. Make him think he had a good time. You're on the next flight home to the Bubble, or I'll find you and cuff you."

Lexie turns and winks at me, then saunters off to the bedroom door and bends to pull on her heels. With Corporal's attention on her, I slap a tiny wireless video camera onto the side of Tremaine's desk.

In the elevator, Corporal turns military, as if he is running a tactical operation.

"Tonight didn't happen. You'll return to work tomorrow, and we will never talk about this."

"Is that what you said to Andrew before he died?"

"I had nothing to do with it."

"Why should I trust you? A guy who was best buddies with Tremaine in university."

"Hexagon started as a student project; a fantasy to build a utopian organization that would look after people's interests in a world that was quickly changing."

"Sounds military."

"It wasn't, back then. Hexagon was an interdisciplinary project between the humanities and business faculties, and it quickly drew the attention of corporate sponsors. The companies guaranteed our entire education up to a doctorate degree, along with comfortable student housing and expense money."

"You sold out."

"We were naive. And poor students. We agreed to the exchange, not realizing that we had traded our autonomy for the interests of a corporation."

I can understand the poor student part. I get that. But would I sell my soul? Even Lexie didn't go corporate; she plays for a jazz band.

"You still have a large share in Hexagon," I counter. "How do you explain that?"

"Tremaine had business acumen from the outset. We formed a corporation. We sold many of our shares to the corporate funders, but we still had a small vested interest that kept us financially comfortable."

"Who's 'we'?"

"Me. Tremaine."

"And?"

He stares me down till I look straight at him.

"Gurman. I saw it on one of the sheets." I point my finger at Corporal as I speak. "Why are you protecting him?"

"He's as innocent as I am."

"You served in the army. You're not innocent." I stride into the elevator that has arrived as we were speaking, and slam the ground floor button. "No one in Hexagon is."

Corporal presses the door close button. "I am," he insists.

"Then why didn't you get out?"

"Our power slowly eroded. The story we were sold was false . . . the controlling interest was in the hands of the corporate funders. We stayed with Hexagon until our educations were completed. After that, we had a vision to reclaim the initial mandate. In time, though, we realized we were fighting a losing battle. With the economic downturn we were forced to stay on, because at least we had a secure income."

"And you didn't care if millions of people died? If the Earth was ruined?"

"I didn't know about the Extinction. Neither did Gurman."

"Bullshit."

"It's the truth. His wife died when . . ."

I wave him off.

"Kenders," he presses. "It all happened so fast. During that time, values changed. Gurman and I wanted to stick to the old ways, while Tremaine planned to climb the corporate ladder. All of the founding members were either voted out or bought out. It was only Tremaine, Gurman, and I who remained."

"What for?"

"I continued my efforts in security operations, but Gurman stayed on only to pour salt on Tremaine's wounds. Tremaine buttered up a group of staunch supporters who elevated him to a powerful position."

"You could have done more on the outside."

"You have no idea what's going on underground. Ask Terk."

21

IT FEELS strange, walking into Andrew's lab when he's not there. Everyone's in the lunch room, and I realize that Andrew never ate here; he always came to see me.

Some of the guys raise their heads when I enter, then return to slurping their soup. I slip onto a cold concrete bench next to Terk, and he pulls a bowl down from the tray for me.

"I'm not hungry," I say in my most despondent voice. I've been perfecting it. I choke on some words, and stutter at other times. Sometimes I'm very angry and loud, or I sob and wail. When I really want to be effective, I drop my voice to almost a whisper.

Terk just nods and says, "It's not tasty, anyway. You'd think they could have added more variety to the menu."

A slight smile crosses my face. "Always the hopeful one, aren't you, Terk."

He glances up from his bowl. "Andrew always was."

I look away. I wish I could trust him, but Andrew warned me. I feel so alone right now. It was never like this during my activism days. It wasn't only Lexie and I; we usually teamed up with animal rights groups, so there was a band of us fighting together. This time, I'm all on my own.

Although I told Lexie a few things, she doesn't know ninety percent of what's going on. Then again, how much do I really know?

Terk quickly changes the subject. "It's a relief, seeing you."

"Relief?"

He nods toward the row of young boys. "Endless training."

But that's not what he means. I think he wants to reach out to me, somehow; he has something to tell me.

I look down the row as the young boys continue to slurp at their chunky bean soup. Their spoons hardly rest on their bowls.

"I feel a deep chill. I'm going to head to bed early tonight," I say.

"How early?"

"Ten."

Our eyes lock, and he says, "You've got thin blood, Kenders."

He smiles, because he understands. "Deep chill" is one of Andrew's code phrases. "Thin blood" is one of the responses. I'm not the only one who spoke in code with Andrew; Terk is privy to certain lines, as well.

If I can trust him.

At this point, though, it's a matter of gathering whatever information I can, and keeping that collection of data well hidden from everyone else. The contents of Corporal's briefcase are stashed in a secret panel in my guitar. I had it built out years ago, when we started our farm raids. They'd never suspect information to be transferred via a guitar. Our roadies were always changing, which offered the perfect opportunity to swap in an activist who could drop in information about the next raid. The panel changed the sound of the guitar, but those muffled tones have become my signature over the years. People have tried to duplicate it by changing strings and chord structures, but they'll never know the real secret.

At precisely ten p.m., I show up at the far corner of the building, and crawl through the dog entrance. Andrew built it for Chopper years ago, and it provided a way to sneak in when Hexagon shut the doors for a routine check. All Andrew or Terk did was implement a "chill"—an override of the surveillance cameras for a few minutes—and show static in the video feed.

I crawl through the opening and walk straight down the long cemented corridor with bare walls and bright lights. I turn the corner and enter into the control room. Terk follows me.

This room was always where I used to come when Andrew was working late. *I miss him.* The "lab dungeon," he called it, but it was the one place where the guys could laugh and be themselves; where discussions weren't monitored. I run my hands along his desk, touching everything: his pens, his books, his framed degree on the wall. Then I see his notebook, and turn to Terk.

"Can I?"

He nods with kind eyes.

I leaf through the pages one at a time, and smile at Andrew's doodles of bees and nature scenes. Other than those, all I see are formulas, not any further clues as to what may have happened. "Can I take it?"

Terk taps on the wall and tugs on a secret panel that opens to reveal rows of books. I gasp, and lean toward them. *Books.* I haven't seen so many since the library was digitized. I reach for a book, flip over the cover, and turn page after page. I read a description of the salamander, rare a decade ago, which has now disappeared along with many other animals following the Extinction. Who would have thought that bees would be gone? Who would ever have expected the world to look like it does now?

I open to another page and stick my nose into the spine. The sweet, musty smell of a book.

"Do you think there are more, Terk?"

He nods. "They wouldn't throw them out. It's their backup; it's just under lock and key. And I'm sure many people have these tucked away in secret spots, like this one." He pulls out a stack of notebooks. "You can take these. They were all Andrew's work. In my opinion, they belong to you."

"Won't anybody . . ."

Terk twists his long fingers in the air. "They were already here. Tremaine and his whole entourage. I gave them one notebook, and they seemed satisfied."

"What was in it?"

He chuckles. "Just time logs. They wouldn't know the difference!"

I sit back in the chair. "What do you think happened?"

He shakes his head and mutters, "Don't know. Believe me, I wish I did."

"What about Corporal?"

"He's got to keep his head above water, answering to Tremaine. They forget about me down here."

I want to ask him more, but I have to be careful. I still need to feign grief, despite my belief that Andrew is alive. I press my fingers against my eyes, and then change the topic.

"I have to find out more about what Andrew was doing. I have to find an answer. Something."

Terk points to the stack of notebooks. "Those are your key. I have no idea what it means, but Andrew was constantly writing in them, talking to himself, making notations. He didn't want a digital trail. He said that sometimes, when you fell asleep, he'd get out of bed and work on this in a corner of your room."

I look away and bunch my fists.

"Man, I'm sorry."

"No, no." I feign wiping my eyes. "It's good to hear someone talk about him. It's like he's still alive. I hate it when people walk past you in the hall, don't even look at you."

"They don't know what to say."

I tap a finger on the notebooks.

"I don't know where to begin." I let out a big sigh. "I can't remember his profs, not even their last names. They understood better than anyone what he was working on. Maybe they can give me a clue as to what happened."

At that suggestion, Terk lifts his finger and walks back to the bookshelves.

"You know how Andrew was . . . he kept every book. I remember he said he ran into one of his profs in the Bubble a few years ago. He said she had written one of these books."

I jump out of my chair and join Terk at the rows of books. I pull each one out and page to the front covers to see if there's a name I recognize. The authors aren't familiar, but the dog-eared pages are. These are the books that cradled in Andrew's arms as he studied, the volumes that rested next to our headboard at night. I sigh, and reach for the next book.

When I am nearing the end of the second row on the shelf, I tap a well-worn navy tome.

"I remember DeMario. She was one of Andrew's favourite profs. A deep thinker, Andrew used to call her. In fact, she's the one who got Andrew a spot at Massey College."

"That's the one he ran into," Terk confirms.

"Where would I start looking for her?"

"He saw her in the church."

"Of all places."

"He said the acoustics carry so far when the organist is practising that a conversation can't be picked up. The prof went there at noon every day."

"Why didn't he tell me about that?"

Terk looks down at his feet, then back up at me. "It was too dangerous."

"Why?"

"Every time Andrew pulled someone from the outside into this project, they disappeared. I wouldn't be surprised if you can't find DeMario now."

22

NIRVANA

The Stick

I'M IN the apple orchard again, the silver moon rising, the grasses scratching the edges of my legs, the crickets calling all around me, every detail as it was last time. Andrew walks up to me with the carved walking stick.

"I made it for you," he says, and tosses it toward me.

I let it drop, and again, he continues to run toward me, pick me up, and swing me around. My heart drops; I was hoping it wouldn't be the virtual Andrew.

We go through the motions: my same questions, his same answers, the apple, etc. I bury my face in my hands. Again, I'm exhausted and confused.

"Kenders?"

His voice interrupts my thoughts.

"Yeah?"

He pushes my bangs from my forehead and looks deep into my eyes, and I'm waiting for him to kiss me, but then he places my hand in his and holds it over the walking stick. He rests our hands there and simply holds mine, not saying anything. This action is something new that he's never done before, and I wait with baited breath.

Andrew starts to lightly stroke my hand, then slips a finger underneath my palm and taps twice, very firmly. I look at him, and his eyes motion downward, toward the stick. It's then that I notice the music staff carved very lightly underneath his initials. A subtle change that only I would see. I lean in to him and cast my eyes down toward the staff again, memorizing the notes. I softly hum the tune, and add in words that I will be able to remember and decode later.

Then he says, "I have to leave now." I look up at him, and he winks at me. "I promise I'll return."

"Do you know when?"

"That's what my late nights were for during the last weeks." A big smile crosses Andrew's face. "Nothing but the best for my fiancée."

My heart drops. It's what he said to me on the night at Madison Square Garden. Now two virtual experiences are colliding and confusing me even more. My Andrew is gone again, and this entity is the pre-programmed, virtual one.

Here we go again. Our fingers stay locked, and then the pressure; the headset pulling me away from Andrew, away from Nirvana, and floating me back to Earth.

23

TREMAINE

Curve Ball

THE EDGE around Paloma's desk is a cork board; not meant for holding memos, but for tossing knives in her spare time. The same boards line her walls. She doesn't have a bullseye, but has painted one red dot in the centre. Hitting anything outside of that is failure, and she prides herself on hitting her mark each time.

"So far, Andrew hasn't turned up anywhere." Paloma flings another knife past Serge's knee, directly into the centre of the target. Serge looks rattled by her skill.

"And we still haven't located his files," Tremaine adds as he paces behind Paloma.

"Where have you looked?" Serge asks.

"We combed through Hexagon's entire system, and there was no trace. He wiped everything clean." Paloma cracks her knuckles. "Anything in the Bubble?"

Serge shakes his head. "Haven't seen him there."

Tremaine's mouth twists to one side. "What about Kenders?"

"We're putting on the pressure, but nothing so far." Paloma tosses the next knife high in the air, and catches it on the dull end of the blade.

"The way I see it, he stole them," Tremaine says, and points at Serge from the opposite end of the room. "If we can't scale up our VR system with a gambling and porn industry, that affects our margins, and your bottom line. Worse, it will soften our control over the masses."

"How, exactly?" Serge inquires. He moves his chair back slightly as the next knife grazes past his knee again, with the same level of precision.

"We know he found out about some of our inner operations," says Tremaine. "There were files disturbed in my private safe."

Tremaine avoids all mention of the Extinction, because Serge is entirely in the dark. As it is, Serge knows too much already.

"Don't you have security cameras?" Serge insists. "Can't you nail him based on that?"

Paloma tugs a knife from the cork board. "There was a malfunction. An entire file was erased on the very night they were stolen. That's why we know it was Andrew. Who else could do that?"

"We'll write it off as a loss," Serge chuckles. "It wouldn't be the first time."

Paloma twirls the knife between her fingers as she says, "That's where you come in. We think Kenders has the files."

"Or knows where they are," Tremaine interjects. "We faked a burned corpse that looked enough like Andrew to fool her into believing he was dead. We hoped she'd go and get his things. She knows his hiding spots."

"Then we set up counselling sessions, so Gurman could get info out of her." From under her leg, Paloma tosses the knife as if she were throwing a curve ball. "You're her friend, right?"

"Yes, but we're not as close anymore. Not since Andrew," Serge responds.

"You know how to get close to a woman," Tremaine grumbles. Unless, Tremaine thinks, Serge is working with them. He curls his lip in disgust. "Turn her head with money–you own the Bubble."

"There will be more built by next year."

Tremaine takes two deliberate steps toward Serge, his arms close to his body as if he is ready to pounce.

"If you make the right moves."

Serge shifts in his seat. "The contract is already in place," he says.

"We know how to break those." Tremaine's voice is now a low rumble.

"Among other things."

As she speaks, Paloma sends two knives slicing through the air, and they land side by side on the edges of the red dot.

"Besides," Tremaine warns as he leaves the room, "you have as much to lose as we do."

TREMAINE EXITS through a side door, then walks down a back hallway and into a room behind the fake window in Paloma's office. "What do you think?" he asks Gurman as he watches Paloma and Serge through the one-way glass.

Gurman continues to scribble a few more notes, then turns off the sound speaker and heaves his heavy body out of the chair.

"Will she trust him?" Tremaine asks.

"I'm not sure. She doesn't talk about much other than missing Andrew."

"Then convince her."

Gurman rolls his eyes. "It doesn't work that way." All Hexagon continues to do is breathe down his neck. No matter how many times he explains the stages of grief, they don't understand that the human psyche doesn't operate like that. It isn't a military operation, wherein everything must go according to some precision clock.

"She'll do whatever the hell we want her to," Tremaine spits back.

Gurman walks closer to the window. "This isn't the Red Door."

Tremaine throws up his arms. "We don't even have one anymore. Before Andrew left, he put a bug in it. We have ten guys working on it, and no one can figure it out. We've had to temporarily cancel the entire project."

Gurman laughs into Tremaine's face. He never agreed with the Red Door, anyhow. No one at Hexagon scares him; least of all, Tremaine. He's a short-sighted man who answers to Hexagon's bean-counters and stakeholders; a man who has to deliver progress metrics each month. For all the power Tremaine projects, he's nothing more than a figurehead and a voice for Hexagon.

Gurman isn't a gopher like that. He has autonomy and freedom. Freedom to look into Tremaine's file and see his jaded history, his foolish mistakes, and his many insecurities revealed in sessions with Hexagon's former psychologist. What Tremaine failed to recognize in his sessions was that everything is recorded, and no one is immune to that. Everything is filed in a digital vault until it can be used against someone.

Tremaine threatened Gurman once, and that was all it took. Gurman now takes every opportunity to pull and scrutinize his file. He watches him in Nirvana and reads through all the virtual reality transcripts, which for the moment are mostly gratuitous sexual exploits, but Gurman is confident Tremaine will reveal something in a moment of lustful pleasure. One line. One word. He will find a flaw, expose it, and remove Tremaine.

Tremaine lifts the back of his wool suit jacket and sits down in the chair. "We need Kenders to get over Andrew and fall for Serge," his gravelly voice idles.

"Grief isn't linear." Gurman's own voice rises in frustration. "It could take years."

"We don't have that kind of time."

"She mentioned a penthouse suite they had years ago. Hexagon put them up there. It's nostalgic for her."

"Book it for her. Whatever she wants, but make sure Serge will be around." A large vein bulges on Tremaine's forehead and runs down toward his temple as he speaks. "We need her to trust Serge and reveal everything."

"How much are you telling Serge?"

Tremaine shrugs. "Whatever he needs to know to get the job done."

"Was that approved by the chair?"

"There's always someone more powerful."

Gurman scribbles notes on Tremaine as he listens: "dissension," "treason," "libel."

Gurman has his own secrets. He doesn't tell Tremaine about half of his sessions with Kenders. Her strange dreams, her knowledge of their operations, her intuitive sense of Andrew. These acknowledgements would only mean more sessions with the woman who interrogates him as much as he questions her. It makes him uneasy, and for his plan to succeed, he has to remain in control. At this point, he isn't sure if Kenders could be important to his ultimate strategy.

Gurman looks back through his notes, then scribbles some more. The truth of the matter is that everyone's life is at risk, not only Kenders'. The intricate Hexagon layers don't overlook anyone's actions or statements. From the files Gurman can access, he sees everything, including Hexagon reports and intelligence surveillance. He is like the spider on the wall, peering in on someone's life, seeing the background, knowing someone's fate before even they are aware of it. But that's where he can play with outcomes; wave his hand over a page with his written notes, and cast someone's life in a different direction.

24

NIRVANA

Warning

I'M PLAYING at Madison Square Garden again, but this time it's different. Lexie isn't here live with me, and I feel like I'm lip synching with her drumbeat.

I am singing the chorus to "Rhetoric," and holding the mic out to the crowd from the suspended walkway so they can join me. I look over at the dance stage, and spot a couple riding their bodies to the beat of the song. I wish that Andrew and I had just been regular teens, and had had this kind of fun. Instead it was always me on stage singing, and him on the research platform with his different agendas. So often our schedules conflicted, and we didn't ever have that period of carefree youth. But now we can't walk away; not after discovering the truth about Hexagon and the bees. If we can, we will fight them.

The couple is now kissing, and I look out into the crowd for Andrew. I am singing the lyrics on automatic, like driving a car, so my full attention is focused on spotting him. That's what the code on the staff said: Madison. So I assumed it was this place; this experience.

As Lexie starts her drum solo, I turn back to the stage to give her the limelight, and I see a familiar freckled face backstage.

Andrew.

I run.

I jump into his arms and press my lips to his so tightly that I never want to come up for air, but I feel him struggling, and he prys me away from his body.

"Sorry," he says, "but I don't have much time. I can only block Hexagon's ability to hack in and listen for so long. It shows as an atmospheric signal interruption, but if it lasts for an extended period, they'll get suspicious."

"Okay . . . but I'm so glad you're here with me!"

"Me too. Listen closely. I only have time to say this once, but it explains everything."

I nod, my eyes wide.

"I found something. Something they'll kill people to keep quiet. Including us."

"I did, too."

"Don't tell anyone."

"I won't."

"Tell me later. They're watching you. Be careful."

"I am."

"I need you to find a holo-disc," he says.

"Where?"

"I have to go. I'll show you here. Meet me at your birthday dinner in Massey College three nights from now."

Just like that, Andrew is gone. I run back out to the stage, looking around frantically.

All I see is the massive crowd everywhere, flicking lights from their holo-watches, and swaying to the music as the lights dim and Lexie starts with her spare and stirring drumbeat. The spotlight finds me, and I walk toward the descending catwalk. The roar from the crowd is a din compared to the thoughts in my own head. I'm looking everywhere for a sign from Andrew. What holo-disc? Where am I to find it here? How will I possibly get the clue?

I walk through the long screens on either side of the catwalk, looking at the images. I start into "Honey," but I don't know where the words are coming from, or how my voice even knows what to do next.

They're watching me. *I knew that.*

They'd kill both of us. *For what?*

Tremaine doesn't even know what we found, unless Corporal told him. But what we know about the Extinction is worth killing us for. I feel guilty singing about it now, knowing that I indirectly played a part in the heinous act. What else am I unaware of? What else is Hexagon hiding?

I stand in front of the first screen with my silhouette superimposed on an image of a field of dead cows.

"Holstein, we still taste you,

Earth, we still need you . . ."

Then I hold the mic out to the crowd and say, "This is your world. Sing the next ones for me."

As the crowd continues to sing my song, calling out the names on the screens I stop in front of, I wonder where Andrew's clue will come from. We're almost done the finale. I'll be leaving this Nirvana experience soon.

And then I look at the screen ahead of me. It shows an image of Chopper on the ground, pawing at his blue bone. It flashes for a brief moment, and then a picture of an eroding river replaces it. I step in front of the next screen, and the crowd shouts out. I look one screen down, and a photo of our backyard flashes, with Chopper's dog house tucked into the corner. Then an image of a flooded Toronto harbour with toppled buildings comes up, and I step in front of it. I salute it with both hands, my mind trying to piece together the two photos of Chopper and what they mean.

The next screen down shows an image of a ravaged forest, and then for a brief second, a picture of me in our living room. I hold an Easter basket in one hand, and lift a pillow with the other. It's gone before I even register the colour of the couch. What does this mean? Chopper and Easter.

I forget about saluting the next image. By now, the crowd isn't even taking my lead. They shout out the chorus before I realize I'm standing still. And then I turn to my left, and see it on the screen: Andrew, holding a leather belt. It hits me in a flash, and I pull all the images together as Lexie's drumbeat crescendos.

The sporadic photos wouldn't mean anything to anyone other than me. Each Easter we hid gifts for each other, and it would only be me who remembered. That particular Easter, Andrew couldn't find one of his gifts: the integral piece for a new outfit that I had hidden throughout the house and our small backyard. I had placed the belt in a plastic bag, and tucked it into the spot where Chopper always hid his toys.

I know where the holo-disc is.

25

I SLIP Chopper a treat so he doesn't notice me creep out the back door and into the darkness. I crawl on the ground, as I don't want any lights detecting me. I feel my way to Chopper's dog run, then inch along it to the space beneath the concrete edge of the patio. I slide my hand under, and find a tiny plastic-wrapped package with a holo-disc. Inside is a note, and I read it frantically:

"The world is crumbling,

You're my distraction from the pain."

They're lyrics from my song, "Diversion." Underneath, he wrote: *Get the picture on my desk, and check the right drawer for a blue package.*

I hide the disc in the panel of my guitar along with everything else, and tuck the note into my pocket. I lean back against the wall. His lab? What will it be next? I have no idea how these items will be a source of deflection, but I've followed his messages this far, so I might as well continue.

I've exhausted all possibilities and contacts I have here in Hexagon quarters to get me in there. And Gurman booked me the room I wanted at the Bubble, but I'm leaving first-thing tomorrow morning. I laugh at the notion. Usually I'd sleep in till noon, and now I'm not sleeping at all. I'm haunted by nightmares, and even when I doze, it's restless.

I take a long shower, and then pack my suitcases and put them in the trunk of my seldom-used car. I'm trying to figure out how I will get into Andrew's lab. Chopper pads behind me the entire time, knowing that something is up. It's uncanny, how animals sense things. I pull him close to me.

"I'm never leaving you behind, buddy."

He licks my face with his rough tongue.

"You're going to visit Lexie. She loves you."

Chopper wags his tail, as if he understands that this is a good thing. All I care is that Hexagon ears hear it.

Yes, I'm visiting Lexie, not Serge. A diversion, if they believe it.

And then Chopper whines with those puppy dog eyes, and I know what I'm going to do.

I have one more stop to make before leaving for the Bubble.

I DRIVE up to the lab facility on the outskirts of the Hexagon compound, and walk up to the security guard.

"Larissa Kenders," he says with a heavy French accent.

"Yes." He knows me by name. Face recognition, or is everyone at Hexagon watching me? "I need to get into Andrew's lab."

"It's in lockdown for the night."

Ah, I see. I feign tears, trying to recreate the sad expression in Chopper's eyes.

"I'm going on a vacation to the Bubble, and I wanted to take his picture with me. He has one of us on his desk." I add some hyperventilation for effect. "I just really miss him."

I sit down, and make sobbing sounds into my closed hands.

"One moment, please."

He walks into the back room, and I hear the echo of words, but I can't make out what he's saying. I hear the guard's drawl, and then another voice. A woman's. *Paloma?* I listen closely, but it's not her. This voice is too high-pitched and squeaky.

While they're talking, I edge closer to the back of the room. No one comes out, so I continue walking down the hall until I hear their voices echoing my name. My heart starts beating. They're looking for me. I hear a door open to the outside. It's my chance.

I dart across the hallway to the back of the building, use Andrew's code to enter his lab, and flatten my back against the wall. It's dark. No one is here.

I creep up to Andrew's empty workstation, take the framed photo, and look around. There's nothing in his drawers. I unfold the note attached to the disc I pulled from Chopper's spot. It says: *Get the picture on my desk, and check the right drawer for a blue package.* Could I have misunderstood? His messages are always so short and open to interpretation.

I pull open the drawer again, and feel along the edge. And then I think of it. I drop to my knees, and run my hands along the bottom. At the very back of the drawer, I touch something hard. I reach farther with my fingers, and pull out a blue triangular pack.

I run to the back of the room, unlatch Chopper's flap door, and crawl through it, just as bright lights shine into the space. *They're looking for me.* I wonder if Andrew knew just how useful the dog door would be when he built it in.

I creep to the front of the building, and sprint toward my car. When I'm two feet away, a loud boom throws me to the ground. My ears are buzzing, but I lift up my head to see the whole building collapsing into one billowing flame.

I wipe the dirt from my face and push myself up from the ground. I am shocked by what just happened. I could have been killed in there if I had stayed a minute longer, all for a diversion.

I shove the frame and blue package into my pocket, and run toward the car. I'm driving off as flames and smoke rise farther into the sky.

26

PALOMA

The Door

ON A holographic screen, Paloma watches Kenders pull the blue triangular plastic package from underneath Andrew's desk.

"That's what we've been looking for."

She slaps her hands together in excitement.

"Where are the exit doors?" Paloma asks.

A second holographic screen appears, showing a blueprint for the building with three separate doors highlighted.

"Pull up the video for each of them," she demands.

A video of the front door pops up, and she watches the static door until flames erupt, glass shards fly into the night sky, and the roof flattens the entire front walkway.

"The next one," she barks.

A video of the back door pops up, and she watches the static door until a blast folds it in two and the second floor slides down onto it.

"The last one." Paloma taps her long red fingernails on the table.

A video of the side door pops up, and she watches the static door until the explosion causes the roof to flatten the entire side of the building.

"Hope you're happy," Corporal growls. "Now she's dead, along with the holo-disc."

Paloma shakes her head, her hoops swaying into her hair. "Go back to the video where she gives us the finger. Where does that hallway lead to?"

"Nothing shows on the blueprint," Corporal says.

"Get me the janitor on the phone."

"He's dead," says Corporal dryly. "Along with another ten people who worked there at night."

"Find me old surveillance footage of that hallway. I want to see where it leads."

"That could take hours."

"Then start now," she barks.

Paloma stares at the package in Kenders' hand as she leaves Andrew's desk. "How did she find out about it? That's a hiding place only Andrew could have told her about."

"She may have known about it before," Corporal suggests.

"No way. She would have gone there right away. Right after we told her he was dead. We've been watching her every move."

"Got her," one of the techs in a back desk says.

"Pull it up," Paloma orders. She walks back toward him, and he bites on his lip nervously as his fingers fly across the keyboard.

"Your name." Paloma circles his desk, taking in the features of this scrawny young boy with a crooked nose.

"Zach."

"Where are you from?"

"Huron."

"What tech talent comes out of Sarnia?"

"A farm boy with nothing else to do . . ." His shaky voice breaks for a moment. "I studied at Waterloo."

"Can you hack the disruptions in Nirvana?"

"I'm working on it."

Paloma leans in front of him, her icy eyes boring into his. "I'm watching you. Do it, and you'll replace Andrew's position."

On the screen, Kenders doesn't leave the office, but walks with the blue triangular pack in hand, unlatches the flap door, and crawls through it.

"She crawled out of there. I knew it!"

"No one could have escaped from that fire in time," says Corporal. "It blasted the whole area in seconds."

"I'm not taking any chances," Paloma replies. "I want all roads blocked. I want that blue pack."

Corporal leans in, inches from her face. "You're not in charge here. I am. And until you show me proof, we're not wasting those man hours."

Paloma doesn't even blink; she just thinks of how Tremaine will flatten him when he finds out.

"By that time, Kenders will be gone," she counters.

"If she's alive, you'll find her. You're Tremaine's bulldog."

"I'm nobody's puppet." She says it deliberately, but she knows that Corporal may be catching on to the pact. He also may be the wild card here. She'll talk to Tremaine about eliminating him. That would give her full reign, and more power.

When Corporal marches out of the room, Paloma slams her fist against the wall. "How did she know we were detonating the building?" She looks suspiciously at Terk.

Terk lowers his head in time, and continues to code along with a row of techs hunched over desks.

Paloma starts pacing again. "There has to be a way Andrew's communicating with her in Nirvana."

"The only thing we've found is a security hack, but that's connected to the Red Door," Zach interjects.

"Work on it," Paloma barks. "It could be related!" She taps on Zach's desk. "In the meantime, record everything in Nirvana. Scrape it twice, and mark the interruptions. If we work through the hack, we want to go straight there. That's where Andrew is talking with her."

27

I SIP a glass of champagne along with other guests while browsing the holographic models of new cars for the 2088 line.

Servers cover the floor with choreographed precision, carrying trays of signature cocktails followed by canapés: skewers of Moroccan-spiced roasted chicken, firecracker rock shrimp wrapped in pastry, beef tenderloin stuffed with sautéed spinach and mushrooms. Each corner of the room is lined with an open bar, and the walls are flanked by dessert tables, carrying everything from cakes, pastries, and a chocolate fountain to a S'mores station, candy buffet, and sundae bar. Not much for a vegetarian, but I focus on the sweets. I haven't seen or tasted food like this for years.

The Bubble is like one massive resort to me: a dome-covered city where people don't see the real, outside world. Residents can choose whether they live ocean-side or garden-view, and illuminated screens and fake landscapes fabricate the experience. As with any resort, only the wealthy live in the Bubble, and a lavish lifestyle overshadows the real-world issues. While the entire country is steeped in food shortages and environmental unrest, the Bubble is still out of touch with reality. Air is fragrant and clean, and people are tanned and healthy, living a lifestyle filled with leisure and entertainment.

A man bumps into me, and I spill my drink. Before I can even grab a napkin, a robotic janitor sucks it up, and when I turn, an automatic mobile bartender has another one waiting for me.

I stand in the corner of the room and watch Lexie on stage, a long skirt covering her ankles, her blonde hair pulled into a chignon. If there's one thing that remains a constant, it's that music can only be performed live, and not automated. There are many ways Beethoven actually intended for his pieces to be played, but they were interpreted with different expressions over the years. Just like Lexie is singing "Honey" right now. We have performed that song with many variances, but we were always belting out the lyrics. I almost don't recognize it at such a slow tempo; the lyrics are emphasized differently as Lexie shortens and lengthens notes, changing the song from how we used to play it. I close my eyes and listen:

"Honey, we still taste you,

Earth, we still need you . . ."

I long to escape to that Madison Square Garden concert in Nirvana right now; to wind back the night to my birthday when I was still with Andrew.

"Was my singing that bad?" Lexie chuckles.

I open my eyes and take in Lexie's new look while we clink glasses. "I didn't know you had such a great voice. Why did I sing all those years?"

"I like drumming better, but now, I have to pay the bills. For some reason, there isn't much interest in punk here, but jazz is big. I've amassed a following." With embarrassment, she points to a life-sized digital board of her on the stage. Lexie in an evening gown, not a slinky black dress. Who would have guessed.

"I'd like to play with you sometime," I say. "I brought my guitar."

"Sure, bring it by anytime."

"I'll have it delivered to your home; my room is small." Lexie can read between the lines. "Do you know DeMario, by any chance? She was Andrew's prof. I just want to let her know that she was always his favourite."

"She's a fan. Usually comes to anything I play at." Lexie prods me through the crowd. "I'll point her out to you."

"I wonder what Tien is doing." She's the only band member I haven't kept in touch with.

Lexie shakes her head. "She was a geek. She went underground."

"What's that?"

"There's Open Source–it's like the public code version of Nirvana. Anyone goes there, can code what they want, do what they want."

"So, what's she doing?"

"It's her second life. She's still a punker there. She's writing lyrics slamming Hexagon. Heard she went to some Bubble in Europe. They actually have NGOs there. More cause-oriented."

"I wish we didn't get split up like we did."

Lexie takes a swig of wine. "It's economics. Here, I get free room and board, at least. And I save on Nirvana fees. Look around you; the Bubble is like a Nirvana, so there's no need to go there."

On that front, she's right. Depending on where you go in the Bubble, you could be in Paris or Venice. So much has been replicated from what Earth used to be like.

Lexie takes a canapé from a tray, and points toward the server as we keep walking through the crowd. "Take him, for instance. He's a robot."

I do a double take; he's so lifelike that I'd never even consider him as a non-human.

I follow him closely, listening to his conversations with people, watching his movements, trying to convince myself that he is not a human and is a machine. I'm pulled away when Lexie taps me on the shoulder as she heads back to the stage. She points to a woman with a thick head of grey hair in front of me.

"DeMario," Lexie whispers.

I walk up to the older woman, my hands shaking. "Prof DeMario?"

She looks up at me with wrinkled pink cheeks. "Larissa?" she asks.

"Most call me Kenders."

She holds out her hand. "I met you once. At Andrew's convocation."

"Yes, yes," I'm quick to answer. I can't believe my luck.

"Where's Andrew?" She places her hand on my shoulder, and leads me away from the crowd.

"Missing." I lower my voice.

She sighs. "All good researchers are."

I'm surprised at this statement of fact. The acknowledgement almost takes my breath away.

"What brings you here?" she prompts. Her dark glasses frame her round face.

"Visiting a friend."

"Enjoy the visit," DeMario says as she shakes my hand again.

I press firmly on her palm. "Can I see you sometime?" I inquire urgently.

"I'm speaking at a conference out west in a few days. Won't be back for two weeks."

My heart sinks. I can't wait two weeks.

DeMario waves to a man across the room, her attention already drifting. Out of desperation I say, "I feel a deep chill."

DeMario turns to me sharply, and our eyes lock. "You've got thin blood," she replies. She writes a quick note on a card, hands it to me, and leaves.

28

I STAND in the middle of the room, watching DeMario slip into a crowd of suits and cocktail dresses. As she fades further from view, I clench her card where she wrote the church address and time, and feel my every hope following her. I wander through the Bubble's presentation centre, carrying my champagne glass through the next hour of empty conversation, forced laughter, and gloating. I'm aware of the cheeriness in the room, the guests unaffected by or perhaps indifferent to the world beyond the protected walls of the Bubble. Do these people know of the state Earth is in, or the conditions people work under in the Farm to produce food?

"By all accounts, 2087 has been a momentous year." The man who speaks from the front of the room is tall, thin, and dressed in a black T-shirt and white pants. "We unveiled our latest peripheral and collected every award possible. Now the buzz has grown so loud that we've received offers from other sectors. Our development has accelerated so dramatically that movie directors have even jumped on board."

The crowd claps while I take a sip of my wine.

"Is he convincing enough?" a familiar voice whispers from behind me.

I shrug and turn toward my old friend, who is dressed in his habitual faded jeans, open sports jacket, and sandals.

"Why aren't you up there?" I ask.

A slow smile breaks across Serge's face, and the dimple curves in his right cheek. "I saw you in the crowd, ma chère."

"What's with 'ma chère'?"

"It's my heritage. I'm French Canadian."

"But you've never talked like that before."

"I just spent half a year in France. Built a Bubble there. I love everything French."

"Is it as bad there as it is here?"

"Yes. Provence is a wasteland. No lavender fields anymore, but the vineyards are still there. Grapevines don't need bees to pollinate. I brought back cases of wine." He gives me a long hug, then clinks glasses with me. "And now that you're here, I want to max out the time I see you. I've got an entire guest suite in my penthouse; why don't you leave your hotel, and come stay with me? I hired a chef and staff from France, and they started today."

"I don't want to put you out."

"I'd love the company." He puts his arm around me. "Besides, there was a rumour you were coming, so I already had my cook make up all your favourites for breakfast. Banana-nut French toast doused in maple syrup."

"You remembered?"

"How could I forget."

A large hologram projects a stage into the middle of the room and draws gasps from the crowd. A booming announcement comes over the loudspeakers: "Part of our promise to you is what the Bubble means for the rest of your lives. We've partnered with Hexagon to bring you the Teleporter!"

The hologram shines bright colours into the air while a team from Hexagon comes on stage.

"Let Don Tremaine, Hexagon's CEO, tell you more."

Tremaine prances onto the stage, preening his hair as he walks. His eyes follow the curves of the hostess in front of him. He turns toward the audience, his snakeskin shoes shining in the spotlight.

"We're trying to be the first to bring the world back to you," Tremaine announces. "We're not going to let you live like those in science fiction novels, with stark surroundings and space-age food bars. Look around you. We've engineered trees and wildlife; food that tastes better than the real thing." Tremaine points to the back of the room. "The group hovering around the canapé bar, don't those tomatoes taste sweet and fresh?"

The people cheer. Tremaine continues, his gravelly voice filling the room. "We've worked with the Experience Lab to transform lobbies and piazzas into safe, social hubs; to create a world for you where nothing is missing from your daily experience." Images of the Bubble complex pop up on a large screen, first the massive dome exterior, then the interior spaces: the beach, the parks, the residences, the community walkways.

"As you know," Tremaine says as he leans over the podium and moves his fingers until the spotlights catch the glimmer from his rings, "at Hexagon, we work hard to protect your world. But we also know you want to journey to the rest of the planet and see how others are living, so we've formed some networks, and are opening Bubble hubs on other continents. This is the first sneak preview."

I turn to Serge. "How did you do it?"

He motions for me to follow him and I smile; it seems like we're back in high school again, Serge the consummate entrepreneur. He had developed his first patent with a friend, the one with whom he had become a millionaire, at the young age of eighteen. Cautious by nature, he developed the idea for a helmet for sensorial isolation after a stressful flight with his parents. Serge had been squeezed between them; his mother had a fear of flying, and his father dominated the video settings so he didn't get to choose any of the entertainment that he wanted. Serge created a system where passengers could program their own music and movies before the flight began. They could also synch their cloud files to a virtual keyboard and monitor that they operated with motion capture gloves. And to filter out his father's constant flatulence, he created a scented ventilation system.

His friend was the programming brain, and Serge, the entrepreneur. He introduced the concept via a crowd-funding site, promising a pleasant economy-class flight. The same day an airline company made him an offer he couldn't refuse, but to his disappointment, they filed the patent and then shelved it, citing aviation regulation difficulties.

A natural entrepreneur, Serge even had plans to create a helmet upgrade that passengers could purchase for twenty dollars per flight, an experience that virtually transported them into the airplane's first class section. He had believed his future to be set, but when his first creation never turned into a product, he vowed from then on to handle any and all production himself.

Serge leads me to the elevator, and as we ascend, he swipes his finger in front of the lower key until an additional floor lights up. I'm watching every move he's making, learning what I can about the Bubble itself. Within seconds, the door opens to a massive lobby, and he turns to me.

"Welcome to my penthouse. Everything here is unique."

"So my hotel room is sub-standard?"

"It's connected via the air vents, so you breathe the same air," he says with a wink. "The best thing is that, here, we can talk without any ears listening in." He points to a mounted camera. "You'll notice there isn't a light blinking on this one."

My eyes widen. "You mean there's monitoring here, too?"

"It's everywhere, but I built this place, so I had my suite designed differently."

I wander into the main living room area, and then into an adjoining library. My fingers trail the spine of each book.

"They're real," I say in surprise.

"Mais, oui. You had an influence on me, ma chère."

"Does everyone here have real books?"

He laughs and leans his lanky body against a shelf. "Digital books. And even there, Hexagon monitors everything people read. If you book-mark a section, if you re-read a page, they know." He shakes his head and chuckles. "All to protect against threats from the Extinction. The perfect control mechanism." He pours me a drink with his typical precision. "But these are old-fashioned paper, and when you've finished reading them, there are more."

"Where?"

"A secret." He winks. "I have to keep your curiosity up so you stay longer."

"You know me. I'll have those read in a week!"

"I'll take you to more, then. In the meantime, you asked about the Experience Lab. Remember my buddy, Phil?"

I nod.

"He was out of work. After the Extinction, Hollywood crumbled and every film director was out of a job, so he came to me. We filmed ev-erything in the dining room; every fork, plate, glass, flower setting, cush-ion, chair back, everything. That data went into our Engine One—we're now up to Engine Fourteen– and we made the Great Room accessible to every Hexagon member."

"Nirvana."

"I built the earliest rendition, and sold it."

"I figured you had a hand in it."

"I lost the contract to another developer, so I don't know what they've done with it since then. But they leased the Bubble from me; that's more lucrative, anyway." Serge lifts a glass to her. "Celebrate with me. We're opening up two more centres."

"What do you mean?"

He opens his arms. "Look at all the children. Population is growing, and we need more Bubbles. Hexagon just contracted two new ones for me to build."

"The same?"

He shakes his head. "This next one is high grade. Full luxury. Pulling out all the stops."

"Where will it be located?"

"Top secret."

"What about the rest of Ontario? Are there any survivors?"

"What could they live on? Nothing's growing anymore. The water is polluted. The fighting over what was left grew ugly. They need Hexagon to survive."

"Hexagon is everywhere now?"

"Yes, and they're not the only power at play. My biggest mistake was selling the Bubble technology to the Westerners. They have more pods than we do here in Ontario. They made a fortune off me." Serge pours another glass of wine. "I learned fast, though. I leased my technology to the States. They pay me royalties, and I control all developments."

"So, you build out their pods?"

He nods.

"Does Hexagon know this?" I press.

"Oui. They control Nirvana, the virtual world, but not the economy anymore. That's over. I built the Bubble, our physical place. The way I see it, they're entertainment, and I'm housing."

"So, where does Hexagon get their money?"

"Do you know what people pay to spend a night in Nirvana?"

"That much?"

"It's a drop in the bucket compared to what stakeholders initially invested."

"Are you one of them?"

Serge nods. "They're a major client. Wish I had more ownership in the company."

29

BREAKFAST IN the Bubble is unlike anything I've experienced in years. Not only is the table covered with platters of food, but each dish is a childhood favourite. I scoop the last bit of a yogurt parfait with fresh fruit, walnuts, and lavender honey from my bowl before considering the next course: a platter of banana-nut French toast drizzled with maple syrup.

I sweep my hands over the chocolate croissants, fruit tarts, and cinnamon buns. "I can't possibly finish all of this, Serge!"

He laughs while he smooths chocolate spread onto his strawberry crepe. "You can stay as long as you want, ma chère; take your time." He lifts up a mimosa glass and toasts: "To you."

I tap my glass to his. "To old friends."

Serge pauses for a moment, smiles ruefully, then turns to the meal on the table.

"Tell me," he asks, "doesn't the fruit salad taste like the real thing? The orange juice? Even the honey?!"

I slip a spoonful of fruit into my mouth and say, "I wouldn't have believed it, but it does. Beats the dry wafers and nutritional shakes Hexagon serves each morning."

Serge's penthouse faces the ocean, and on his balcony the entire salt-water experience is simulated with misting nozzles and scent dispensers in the walls, and heat blowers and fans in the ceiling and floor. As I sip my freshly-squeezed orange juice, the warm sea breeze and the ocean mist brush against my skin. The fans blow my hair into my face, and Serge reaches over to brush the bangs from my eyes.

My suitcase is still sitting in my hotel room where it was delivered, and I need to get back there, but I also need to know if I can trust Serge. I'm not sure how to start the conversation, so I just blurt it out.

"I need your help."

"Another pig farm to liberate?"

I heave a deep sigh. "This is more serious. And I don't know where to turn."

I tell him everything, and he sits back and listens, hands shifting, eyes skeptical.

"There's something Andrew needs me to find here."

"How do you know it's him talking to you in Nirvana?"

"No one else knows the things he does."

"Maybe he uploaded his brain."

"I don't think so. He never believed in that."

"This is risky, Kenders."

"I know. I shouldn't have asked you. It affects your business." What was I thinking? Bringing down Hexagon affects him as a stakeholder. I'm getting too desperate to think clearly.

His mouth closes in hurt. "I've never put my business before you," he counters. "Who gave you inside information and helped you close down that live seafood market chain? I was a shareholder there."

He's right. In broad daylight, we removed all the crayfish from a live seafood market, and released them back into the waters from which they were originally captured. They were in deplorable conditions; wounded with missing limbs and claws, stacked on top of each other in crates without access to water. The lobsters came next.

"This is much bigger, though."

"I'll do anything to help you," Serge says as he folds his hands over mine. "I always have. But I need to know: is this what you want, or is it for Andrew?"

The question stops me cold. I haven't had a moment to think about it in the last few weeks. It's been such a blur. Of course, I was a part of averting the Red Door program, but I have no idea what's at stake here. I tug my hands away from his, but he holds on with surprising force.

"Are you saying I shouldn't trust Andrew?" I demand.

"I'm saying you're getting in too deep." He looks at me with concern in his eyes. "Where I might not even be able to help you."

"What if Andrew has found something that can change things?"

"Nothing will ever change long term. You can topple powers for a while, but they always resurface. It's the way of the world."

Does he have a point? The seafood market we closed down opened up under a different name the following year. The university labs simply moved their facilities. Deep down, I agree with him. But I will never tell him that. And I won't ever stop trying to change the world, to make it better, if only for a few. If I give up hope, then what is living for?

"I can't resign myself like people in the Bubble do. It's not reality."

"It's my reality. It could be yours."

"The Bubble seems like one big Nirvana. It's all simulated without even pulling a headset on."

Serge releases my hands. "Maybe it is. Why are you clinging to the way the world was, when it doesn't exist anymore? I mean, look at our Earth!"

"It's better than Nirvana."

His fingers brush my hand for a moment. "You could be here. Start your life over. I'll get you top billing in the best clubs. A record deal."

I lift one shoulder and shrug. "If you're right, then I've played at Madison Square Garden virtually. I've lived that dream."

"Is that why you want to marry him? He can create any fantasy for you?" Serge's hazel eyes cloud with hurt.

I'm shaken to the core. I don't want to beset my oldest friend. Till this moment, I never thought I could. We have been friends for so long, but Serge always wanted more. And I didn't want to damage that relationship, the only family member I felt I had.

"You could have it all with me." Serge places his hands on the table to get up, and it lowers slightly under the weight of his arms. "But that's not enough for you."

He walks to the balcony, and I don't follow. How can I explain what draws me to Andrew? He has such a hopeful outlook, and he's always working to better the world, rather than his pocketbook.

I look up at Serge, so small against the wide ocean in front of him. He appears trapped by his emotions in the corner of his balcony, like a caged animal. I lift a hand and hold it to my own chest. Am I any different than the hunters I fight against, who pen animals as commodities? Would I ask this favour of any other friend, or am I commodifying Serge's devotion to me? I can't ask this of him. It's unfair and cruel.

Slowly, I get up and walk to the elevator. I have to do this alone.

30

I LIGHT one candle, and then another, until I have nothing else left to do but sit in a pew. I haven't stepped inside a church for so long, I'm unsure of the protocol.

I listen to the organ music till it stops. Then I hear footsteps, the creaking of an old wooden pew, a woman's cough, and the shuffling of her jacket. I don't look right away; I'm sure I've raised enough suspicion by even coming to the church.

Instead, I wander through the aisles. The building is an exact replica, right down to the tower and spire that rise three hundred and five feet above the street. It's what people had wanted—the life they once had—and Serge delivered. It's what he's good at: giving people what they want. He's a salesperson and a visionary.

Serge. He's the one person who truly cares for me, and I've closed the door on him. I stop in front of the stained glass window on the northeast side of the Chancel, looking at all the images of people tending the sick, sheltering the homeless, feeding the hungry. Is that now Serge's responsibility? He has taken such an interest in my wellbeing, should I be hiding from him? He could potentially help me.

I see DeMario from behind. The sun slips through the window, and reflects off the sunglasses perched on the top of her head. Her grey hair is tied into a ponytail, and one arm is resting on the back of the pew. I slide in beside her, and DeMario uncrosses her legs so I can pass, then lowers her arm with a polite nod and motions for me to sit.

"Not many people come here mid-day," she says as she taps her foot on the floor nervously.

"I heard the organist is very good," I reply in a hushed tone.

"Mmmm."

We exchange glances and smiles, then look forward for a while. She's silent and I wonder if she feels I'm stalking her. Terk told me this was her noon respite, but she did write it on the back of her card.

"Andrew showed me your picture every time." DeMario crosses her legs again. "He was my best student. So bright. So inquisitive. And then . . ."

"It halted all of our lives."

"Yes. You're a musician, right?"

"Yes."

"I saw you once. At the university pub." She lowers her voice. "What happened?"

Suddenly I feel the pressure of this situation, the weight of being all alone, and I press my lips together to fight off the tears.

"Andrew's gone. Hexagon says he stole files." I hesitate and then stop, wringing my hands in my lap.

DeMario averts her eyes and is quiet. It unnerves me, and makes me feel as though I've made a mistake. Eventually she asks, "Why are you telling me this?"

"I need your help."

"Andrew said the same thing the last time he saw me here."

"What for?"

"It's complicated."

I open a hymn book, planning to subtly slip one of Andrew's notebooks into it to show DeMario, then wonder if there are cameras.

"I have his notebooks," I say. "All formulas. I was hoping you could tell me if there are clues in them."

"Clues?"

"To find him."

DeMario lowers her round glasses onto her nose, and looks over the hymnal at me. "I can't look at them here. You understand that."

I nod.

"When you leave," she continues, "you will get up to look at a statue, then walk out, forgetting your purse in the pew. Walk straight down the alleyway so that when I run out into the courtyard to give it to you, you will be gone from my sight. I will take it home, remove the books, then call the Bubble to have them deliver your purse."

"Okay."

"Come here tomorrow, and I'll tell you what I find."

I nod, relieved that she'll have a look.

"When did you last see him?" DeMario inquires.

"In Nirvana, if that counts."

"Why wouldn't it?"

"It's not real."

"Did it offer you comfort?"

I nod.

"Then it's real," she affirms.

"But, it was in Nirvana."

"Just because you're not in your physical body, doesn't mean the things you experience aren't real. Think of your dreams. Your feelings. You still love Andrew?"

I bite on my lip and nod.

"Then," she continues, "that love is still real, even though he isn't physically here."

She has a point. I smile ruefully at DeMario, then deliberately knock my purse to the floor as I leave.

AS I walk through the synthetically fresh air from the church back to Serge's penthouse suite, ignoring the many offers of rides from the limousine taxis that crowd the streets, I recall my last conversation with

Andrew. So many days have passed since I last saw him.

Suddenly, I start to run as I see the flash of a man who has the same hair crossing a crowded bridge. I race up the stairs, my heart pumping as I push past people. Out of breath, I reach the man and grope for his arm, practically pulling him to the ground. The man spins around, and the face of a stranger looks back at me.

"Let go of me!" The man's green eyes pierce mine with an angry stare. I turn my head, embarrassed, and walk away.

What has happened to me? I'm not thinking straight, running up to a complete stranger. I slump into a bench in the park. I know what I need to do next, with or without Serge's help.

31

I ENTER my hotel room quickly, and survey every corner. I watch a red light blink on the camera, and know I'm being watched.

I stake out the room. Nothing out of the ordinary here; it all looks the same as when we stayed here the last time. A comfy sofa near the sliding door, a bistro set on the balcony. I consider the dresser. Should I unpack my clothes, or just leave the suitcase sitting bedside? There's nothing valuable in it. Everything of worth is stored in the secret panel of my guitar, and that's safe with Lexie.

I place my suitcase in the closet, and sit on the chair for a moment. What happened to this world? *Focus, Kenders.* Andrew wants me here, in this room, so where am I to find what I'm looking for? I don't want to turn the place over, and alert a security guard who might be watching the tape. All Andrew said was where we made love. That means the bed.

The covers look inviting, and I pull them back. I sink into the bed, bend an electronic newspaper over my knees, and pretend to be reading. While I swipe at the pages, my other hand feels around the mattress, but there isn't a zipper or an opening. I pull a small knife from my pocket and peel back a corner, but I still can't find anything. I have no choice; I need to do this in front of the cameras.

I peel back the sheets, and slice deep into the mattress. There, between the box springs, I see a small disc. I snatch it up, and stuff it into my pocket.

I'm lifting the sheets from the floor when Corporal bursts through the door.

"Get out, they're coming," he shouts. He opens a vent in the ceiling, grabs me around the waist, and hoists me into it with a grunt.

"Crawl through this. It will take you to Serge. Go." He replaces the vent cover, then throws a lamp at the balcony's sliding glass door, breaking it with a loud shatter.

A few seconds later, Paloma barges through the door, and I freeze. Through the slats in the vent, I can see everything.

Paloma cases the room. "Where is she?" she demands.

Corporal feigns searching. "Not here."

She looks down at the slashed mattress, then back at Corporal. "She got something."

Corporal shakes his head. "She's just freaking out. Panicking." He lifts up the fluff from the mattress. "It's all just feathers."

She takes a step closer to him, and holds a knife under his chin. "You're lying."

"Paloma." His voice is resolute. "Try me." He steps toward her.

They're out of my vision now. All I can hear is arguing and shuffling. I'm worried for Corporal, and I want to move to get a better look, but I can't risk it. If there is any sound, if they find me, she will kill us both. And whatever Andrew needs from this disc will be gone forever.

"Why didn't you stick with us? You could be so rich. So powerful," Paloma cajoles.

"The same reason Andrew didn't," Corporal states flatly.

"We gave him too much autonomy. Equipped him with the machinery and automation he needed. Funded all of his research."

"The lab explosion. Was it an accident?"

"It was planned." Paloma smirks.

"I never trusted any of you." Corporal's voice is growing louder. "But you needed us."

Paloma lets out an eerie laugh. "You and Tremaine are dispensable. Gurman is next. I don't need anyone."

She pushes him to the floor. All I can see are Corporal's boots, one pant leg pulled above his grey sock, and her heels beside him. Those same shoes every time. Black, with red heels.

I hear the heavy footsteps of another person, and then a muscled guy steps into view. He has short black buzzed hair, and a Hexagon tattoo at the back of his neck.

It's the thug who removed me from my home. He picks Corporal up by his ankles, and he dangles like a rag doll. He looks to be in such a vulnerable position; so weak in his curled up state. The guy starts to swing him. Corporal has to weigh two hundred and fifty pounds, at least. Who is this thug? Maybe he's one of those digital machines.

"Anything else to tell us?" Paloma's voice is loud and brash. "Or do we just kill you now?"

Corporal's face is starting to turn red, but his expression remains resolute, as if he's not bothered in the least, as if he's in another place already. And maybe that's it. He knows where this is going, and he's already detached himself from what's coming.

"I'll make him talk," says the thug.

He drops Corporal onto the floor, ties his legs to a chair, then grabs a finger and snaps it. I hear the crunch, and I know it hurts, but nothing changes in Corporal's face.

"Break his whole hand," Paloma says.

I can't let it happen, but I don't know what to do. I don't even know where I am, or how I'll get out of here. I know I'm breathing harder, and I press my mouth into my arm. I gasp into my skin, closing my eyes for a moment to try and calm myself down.

Corporal will know what to do. He's been in far more dangerous positions.

"I wouldn't tell you anything." Corporal's voice is weak but he continues, "Even if I knew where she went."

I open my eyes to see what happens next. Paloma calls out to her thug, "Go after her," and points toward the broken glass in the sliding door. "I'll take care of him," she adds.

Now I know why Corporal broke the glass. He made it look like I escaped that way; he was blowing them off my trail.

The thug snaps and twists Corporal's hand till it dangles from his wrist, and then leaves. Paloma remains, looking around the room. For a moment she even looks up, almost right at me. If she finds me now, I'm dead. Suddenly, there's a rustle outside, and something drives her attention to the balcony.

She digs a heel into Corporal's body. "You were so cocky before," she gloats. "Blaming me for everything. You were a reckless twenty-year-old when I met you. Some naive kid who thought he could change the world. And look at you now."

Corporal says nothing. What is he thinking? It's him against her now. In any other circumstance he could take her on with one arm.

She points her knife toward his head and says, "You know what we're really doing. But guess what . . . it all dies with you right now."

She pauses, and a sick smile crosses her face.

"I've been waiting for this moment for a long time."

One flick of her hand, and the knife slices straight through Corporal's chest. His head drops, blood gushing to the ground.

Paloma heads out to join her thug, pausing to look back and smile at what she's done.

I want to scream, but I can't. I can't risk it, not after Corporal gave his life to protect me. I fight back the tears. Why me? Did he know that what I have is that valuable?

I stay here for a long time, not sure what to do, not sure whom to trust. My last ally is dead. I thought I couldn't trust Corporal, but he was the only one I *could* rely on. Now who do I turn to? He had mentioned Serge . . . was he working with him?

I remain still until I'm sure no one is coming back. I can't drop back into the room; there are surveillance cameras everywhere. Panic sets in, and then I remember that Corporal had told me to crawl toward the opening. I start to shuffle my body down the passage when a hand clamps on to my foot.

32

THE HAND tightens on my foot, and a voice whispers, "Stay still, Kenders." It's Serge. He places a mask into my hand, and I pull it over my head.

I tug it into place and take a deep breath of clear air. And then I hear his voice from inside the mask.

"I'm going to get you out of here, okay?"

"Okay," I say weakly.

"Let your body go limp so I can pull you."

He talks softly to calm me the whole time he drags me. I can remember the office we gassed years ago to put security guards to sleep, so we could break into the monkey lab. The entire operation was orchestrated remotely, with Serge talking us through the dark hallways, telling us where to turn. Now here he is again, his calm voice in my head when I'm about to crack under what I just saw.

I collapse on the floor as he pulls me through the vent and back into his home. My brain is a daze. Corporal is dead. Paloma's hunting me down. But what for? What is at stake for these people, to cause them to go to such dark lengths?

I reach into my pocket, and grab on to the disc. What do they want so badly from it?

Serge drapes a blanket over my shaking body. "Here." He hands me a glass. "Drink."

I can't even hold the glass, so he places it next to my lips. I just open my mouth, and he pours the liquid in. I can hardly swallow; my throat tightens at the thought of Corporal's bloody body. Serge was right. I'm in over my head.

My bangs are plastered to my forehead, and Serge brings me a cool cloth. "Come and sit," he says, gently guiding me with his hands.

I lean into his body, feel his strong arms around me, and start to quiver. Tears come for the first time, fast and furious, and then my entire body cries out in anguish.

I've been tough, I've led riots that broke into buildings, but I've never experienced this kind of violence. Sure, I've seen butchered animals on the floor in a meat packing plant, and mangled foxes that attempted to chew off their own feet from within a trap, but I've never seen someone killed in front of me in cold blood. I feel vulnerable, and entirely out of control.

I begin to shake, despite Serge's hands rubbing my back. But then his voice is in my ear, whispering softly. It grounds me. And then his lips are on my cheek. Then on my lips.

For a moment, I'm lost in the feeling of wholeness. Of belonging. Of being rooted in something I know.

Comfort.

And then I see Corporal's bloody body in front of me, and I start to shake again.

Someone died because of me. It eats me up inside. I feel like shards of glass are splitting my head open. The guilt.

And then I think of Andrew. And here I am, in the arms of someone else; in the arms of Serge.

I pull away.

"I just . . ."

Serge puts a finger on my lips to quiet me. He runs his hand along my jaw, then the side of my face.

"I know." His whole heart is in every word. "I know."

I put my hand on top of his, and hold it to my cheek. Serge has been there for me my entire life. And then it hits me.

"No, no." I suddenly shoot up in a panic. "I can't stay here. You'll be dead next. I'm going to go."

"Where?"

"Hexagon." I hurry toward the elevator, and Serge stops me.

He grabs on to both my shoulders and says calmly, "You can't go back there. If you stay here, with me, I can protect you."

"For how long?"

"The rest of my life."

Our eyes lock, and for a moment I find myself torn between friendship and love, something for which there is no name. *Serge.* It tugs at my heart.

And then I see Andrew's face, and my chest explodes in a sob.

I sit down and catch my breath.

"Why didn't you tell me what you were doing?" Serge asks.

"I tried to."

He hangs his head. "I'm so sorry. I was caught up . . ."

I touch his hand, which is surprisingly warm.

"I know," I say. "There's something about us . . ."

"And then there's nothing about us," he says sadly. "Forget about that now. I want you safe."

"I won't ever be safe. I'm a target."

"I'll help you. Just like I did years ago."

"You've already done too much," I mumble.

I'm still shaken by what I've seen. I've lost Corporal because he was trying to protect me. I won't have it happen to the only other person here, physically in my life, who cares about me.

"You'll never be a target as long as I'm alive," Serge says gently. "I'll always stand by you. Just like I did back then."

"I need to fight them. Do it differently."

As I say it, I see my life in a different light. What I've lived for until now—the fights, the causes—they were all just chasing anger. Dislodging my own demon that has been lurking within me for all these years. Since that time when I was eight years old, I've been fighting; standing up for the innocent.

But has my passion caused a ripple effect of damage? Are there innocent people whom I affected when I stormed farms, ransacked labs, or shut down stores? Did people lose their jobs? Did their families lose their homes? I never considered these possibilities when screaming fans were egging me on. We were collectively seduced by a cause. It softened our anger, if only temporarily.

Now I'm thinking about the implications, because I'm sitting on the other side. I have a group of people storming down my fence, with no one in my corner but Serge and Lexie. And a virtual fiancé, who appears once in a blue moon for a few moments.

Serge takes my hands in his. "Who else can help you here like I can?" he asks. "I built the Bubble. I have access to areas no one else even knows about."

He argues his case well. "If you help me," I say, "you have to make sure it doesn't hurt your business."

"Since when did you become a capitalist?" he smirks.

"I'm trying to see both sides."

"Don't get soft on me," he says. "We're just starting a fight here."

I force a smile.

"If I help you, you have to tell me everything." His eyes burrow into mine.

"I did tell you everything."

His eyes turn hard. "What did you get from the mattress?"

If I can't trust Serge, then who is left? I swallow the fear lodged in my throat, then take a shaky breath and hold his gaze. I have to face this.

"A disc."

I reach into my pocket, pull out the device, and hand it to Serge.

"This is old technology." He turns it over between his fingers and shakes his head. "They haven't used memory sticks since 2030."

"Can you access it? I have to know what's on it."

"No, but I know someone who can."

"Who?" I take the device back into my own hands.

"DeMario."

33

NIRVANA

Massey College

I ENTER the Nirvana system through my watch, and am relieved to discover that I still have access. I was worried that I would not be able to work it out on my own, but Andrew has made it simple for me to come to Nirvana from anywhere.

I stand in front of the wooden staircase for a while, and run my hands along the banister. I think of all the times that Andrew and I had touched this very wood without a second thought for the significance it could hold for us, and for how the world might change within a few years.

I walk up the grand steps of the foyer, holding on to the wooden banister, my thoughts on the Wisdom Windows in the Upper Library. I look at each of the nine stained glass panels. Every detail is here. I know them well; each image, each word.

I stop at the farthest corner and read the words of Ursula M. Franklin about Light, Enlightenment, and Innovation: "It is no wonder that the boundaries between zones of darkness and places of light—the transitions, shadows, and eclipses—have provided and continue to provide the most profound insight."

"We need the light to see the darkness, and in the darkness is the truth." Andrew had told me this one evening when we were sitting in the courtyard. We called it his Quadrangle Mantra. It became the founding idea behind Andrew's thesis. It was his personal mission statement.

A wave of sadness washes over me. Here, in the halls that we walked, in the rooms where Andrew developed his theories and philosophies, I feel the painful loss of him more than in any other place. Will I ever see him again?

"Care to dine with me?"

I turn to see Andrew, dressed in a suit and tie, with a flower bouquet for me.

"What's on the menu?"

"Coriander and mustard seed tofu with phyllo vegetable bundles."

Absolutely every word is the same as last year when Andrew created this special dinner for me at Massey College, but I slip my arm through the crook of his elbow. We step into the private dining hall and seat ourselves close to the north wall. I stare at the portrait of Robertson Davies that hangs there.

"He was the Founding Master of Massey College, until 1981," I murmur.

"I remember you reading *World of Wonders*," Andrew recollects.

"*What's Bred in the Bone*," I add.

Andrew has a mischievous glint in his eyes, and then raises his wine glass.

"Happy Birthday, Kenders."

I smile wistfully. He always made each birthday so special. I kiss his lips, and hold on to the feeling in my mind. I'm so glad Andrew asked me to meet him here, in this saved experience of ours where we were together. I've been needing to spend a longer length of time with him, even if it is with his virtual self.

Andrew nods to a corner, and Beethoven starts playing.

"I couldn't fit your favourite punk band into this small room," he jokes.

I laugh in delight.

Andrew looks at me. "Sixteen."

I turn to him, hoping it may be my real Andrew for a moment. I say, "Almost eighteen now."

My heart sinks when there's no change in his expression. He continues to run his hands along the curve of my shoulders.

"Robertson Davies has the next birthday surprise for you."

Virtual Andrew. He'll have to do for now, and I watch him as he proudly explains his new developments to me.

It had been a night full of all my favourite Canadian authors who had graced Massey College over the years. Andrew had encoded their voices, physical features, and expressions from public readings and lectures they gave. If I asked a question, they'd answer, lifelike and true to form. It was all in the code, generated from past conversations, books, and movies. It was all he could do for earlier authors, who hadn't uploaded their brains.

I sigh, and turn my attention back to the conversation.

Andrew's smile is ear to ear. "This is the world as you know it."

Davies looks up for a moment, and then says, "The world you report is rarely more than half the world you know."

I turn to Andrew and say, "We should put him into my Madison concert."

Andrew only prompts me to shake Davies' hand.

Virtual Andrew. Still.

And then he says the most uncanny thing, given what I know now: "The corporation funds it, they control the info, they own the rights."

All that time ago, Andrew knew the dangers.

Andrew turns to me sharply. "Kenders, it's me."

I throw my arms around him. "I got the holo-disc from our backyard."

"Good."

"What's in it?"

"Everything about the Red Door." He cups my face in his hands. "Did you get the frame on my desk?"

I nod.

"There's a holo-disc in there, too," he whispers in my ear. "Listen, I only have a few seconds. They're getting better at tracking. Torrance. Go there."

In that instant, my real Andrew is gone, before I can ask him about the holo-disc from the lab, or the memory stick from the hotel room.

I sit through the rest of the dinner, talking with other authors and musicians, hoping that Andrew might return.

What sticks in my mind, though, is the comment Andrew made about Hexagon owning the rights in virtual. If Andrew has coded himself into virtual reality, if we all have, do they control that? Can they wipe out this very experience I'm in, or Andrew himself? If I never see him again, he potentially is lost to me forever.

Andrew doesn't come back.

Torrance.

I know exactly where he wants me to go.

34

SERGE SHAKES his head. "He wants you to go where?"

"Torrance."

"That's leaving the premises. I can't protect either of us out there."

"It's a virtual experience back in Nirvana, not the actual Torrance Barrens. I don't even know if that still exists."

Serge taps his finger on the edge of his knee. "Are you sure it's Andrew who's talking to you in Nirvana?"

"Definitely."

"How can you be sure?"

"I *know* Andrew."

"It could be a trap set by Hexagon."

"To draw Andrew in, and then kill him?"

"Not even exclusively Hexagon. If what Andrew knows is important enough to kill for, there could be many other people who would want their hands on the same information."

I had never thought about that. How naive. Andrew isn't the only programmer in the world. Someone else could figure out a way to hack into Nirvana. It could be anyone playing with me. If Corporal has died for nothing, I'll never forgive myself. What have I done?

I go back in my mind over the messages that Andrew has sent me.

"Only he knew about Chopper's hiding place," I reason.

"Okay, so that's Andrew, but maybe someone is just watching till you gather everything from Andrew, and then they'll come in to collect. You mean nothing to them. You're just a courier in their eyes."

"Then we let Hexagon think we duplicated the discs. And pass the information out so they know I'm not the only source."

Serge nods. "Who can we trust to hold that bluff?"

"I know the perfect person."

I GAG inside when Tremaine stops in his tracks as Lexie drops her sunglasses. I insisted on being in the cabana behind her lounger, to see him fall. And in case anything goes wrong.

"Let me get that for you." Tremaine picks them up and sits down next to Lexie on the well-placed empty lounger. He motions for his entourage to carry on.

Lexie leans forward to grab them, her untied bikini top dropping slightly, and she giggles as she pulls it up. *A few years in the Bubble, but she hasn't lost her touch.* One time, when we needed some intel on the inner workings of a company, we accepted a gig for a birthday concert for the CEO's teenage son. Lexie went to check out the "venue" ahead of time, and got all the information we needed from the lustful father.

She looks Tremaine over, smiles, and says, "I thought you were at Hexagon?"

Tremaine struggles to find a voice and peel his eyes from her chest. "I have a condo here, too. Am down for a board meeting."

Lexie leans back in her chair and moans. "I just love the warm sun." She looks over at Tremaine, batting her eyelashes. "Don't you?"

All he can do is nod and lean back, even though he's dressed in a full suit. *Sucker.*

"How about dinner?" he asks as he preens his hair.

Lexie flashes her best smile. "At your place?"

Tremaine can hardly collect himself off of the floor, and just nods. *Damn, she's good at this.*

"I'll have to take a rain check. I'm waiting for the latest media gossip."

"What?"

"Don't tell anyone." She leans in. "It's top secret, but apparently there's some news about the Extinction threat."

"What kind?"

Wait for it . . .

"The buzz is . . ." She scrolls through her tablet and reads. "It says right here that some evidence was found."

She places the article within eye's view of Tremaine while she takes a sip of water. Then she takes it back from him and continues to swipe to the next page.

"It's a media friend of mine. She says there's some evidence. On a spreadsheet that she has." Lexie leans back in her chair and adds, "I'll let you know what I hear, but I'm sure it will be in the papers before long."

Tremaine can hardly find his voice. "Please do," he finally stammers.

Stinger.

Now the next move is mine.

35

I WALK down the street of the Bubble, afraid Paloma's thugs are on my tail. I've disguised myself as best I can, but I can't help the feeling that everyone is looking at me, everyone is wondering who I am. Did I dress too conspicuously? *I should have worn a different top. I should have worn the black wig.* I question everything I've done.

A man bumps into me, and I jump.

I should act more calmly. I'm reacting as if I'm guilty. *Don't look so suspicious.*

Change. *Change.*

Slow my walk down. Slow my walk down.

Smile back when people smile at me.

Look. Look confident.

Don't smile too much, though. *Not too much.*

All I need to do is make it into the church to see DeMario. It's all I need to do. Five blocks to go; I can see the church ahead of me.

Every step feels like a countdown. Every step. Serge is talking to me through my ear piece. He sees me on a camera. Every step. He tries to calm me down. He talks to me softly.

"Walk slower," he says. "Walk slower."

Then I see someone. A thug from Hexagon. The same one who tortured Corporal. I walk faster. Faster.

Serge speaks firmly into my ear piece. "Slow down." Then again, more firmly. "Slow down. He's following you."

I keep walking quickly. It's all I know. It's the only thing I can do. I need to do something.

Serge is screaming to me through the ear piece, but I can't help it. "What are you doing?" he demands. "People are looking at you!"

I walk faster and faster, because the thug is coming closer and closer to me.

I can hear Serge breathing rapidly. His voice is quick and sharp. "What's up? What's up? Tell me what's going on."

I turn a corner. The thug turns.

I walk faster, my heart racing.

I turn right, dart into an alleyway, and start running. I see a door frame, and duck into it.

Wind funnels through the tight corridor, and I can't hear a thing. I have no idea if he's creeping up on me right now.

It's dark, and I wait.

In my ear piece, all I hear is Serge, but I can't answer him; I don't know if the thug is right behind me. I have to shut him out, or Serge will distract me.

I focus on the thumping of my heart. My heavy breathing. My wild thoughts.

"Kenders!" Serge yells, so loudly I worry someone in the alley could hear his voice. "Say something. Anything."

I can't. I don't know if the thug is out there, waiting for me to emerge. I have more patience than him. I'll wait it out.

I've done this before. Years ago, when we blockaded University Avenue by Queen's Park, the police broke us up. I ran and split down an alley to avoid detection. I waited it out, just like I'm doing now. I'm good at this.

🐝

BY THE time I enter the church, I wonder if I'm putting DeMario in danger as well. Should I be meeting her ? Organ music fills the church, and I see her grey ponytail bobbing on the back of her black jacket as her head moves with the music. I slip into the pew.

"Andrew touched upon something powerful in his research." DeMario gets right to the point.

"So wouldn't Hexagon want to find him?"

"It wasn't what they wanted him to discover." There is a tinge of sadness in DeMario's voice. "Hexagon doesn't help research, they control it. I only know from colleagues in Agriculture who were involved in an interdisciplinary research program funded by Hexagon. They had to provide monthly reports, and it was determined which direction they would pursue. My one colleague, very principled, insisted that he follow a certain direction they weren't approving. They pulled his grant, and he lost his position the following year."

"Where is he now?"

DeMario just sighs. "Manfred Oblick. He never came back to academia. He ended up moving way up north."

"What do you think happened?"

"He got too close to the truth. When he disappeared, Hexagon deflected any suspicion. They funded research grants to explore the decline of the bees, mentioning how important it was for their mandate to end world hunger. Oblick's research pointed accusations toward an agricultural pesticide Hexagon had developed, and they would have become a leading suspect in the bee deaths. It would have undermined their entire operation. Hexagon redirected attention to a class of chemicals called neonicotinoids. Several countries imposed bans on neonicotinoids, and scientists increasingly looked into the areas Hexagon was funding."

"Why would the university turn a blind eye?"

"They can't exist without funding. Scientists can't continue their research or run their labs without corporate dollars. Everything is controlled." DeMario speaks in very clear, succinct tones. "What you have here is worth killing for."

"For who?"

"Hexagon. They control everything with food production. Andrew found a way to bring back the bees."

My throat locks up for a moment. "How?"

"It's complicated. There's work that needs to be done, but he has the formula. Everything is here. He started it."

It's monumental.

"There are things that are missing, but from what I've read in his notebooks, he's found a way," DeMario concludes.

I don't tell her about the holo-disc. Not even the memory stick, like Serge wanted me to. I don't trust anyone right now, and knowing what I am holding in this disc, what Andrew left for me, I can't risk it. Maybe DeMario works for them, too. Maybe she's a plant to get it from me.

DeMario speaks slowly. "Don't mention this conversation to anyone. Not even your friend Serge."

"Why?"

"I don't trust him."

I shoot DeMario a surprised look.

"He uses his technology for money, not the greater good of the people. I think he's just like Hexagon," she continues.

"I've known him since we were kids," I argue. "I trust him."

"And how long have you known Andrew?"

"Three years."

"And you trust him, too?"

I feel my eyes narrow.

"Are you saying I shouldn't?"

36

I WALK into Serge's home quietly, not wanting to even look him in the eye. I didn't hand over the disc, and now I have a warning about him from DeMario. I'm not sure what my next move should be.

I plan to sneak into my room, fake tiredness, and sleep all day till I figure out what to do, but when I'm halfway down the hall, I hear voices in hushed tones, and I follow them.

The inflection of Serge's voice draws me closer. I walk quietly, heel to toe, one small step after another, closer to the library.

I hear another voice. Male. I've heard it before. Tremaine? *No.* Not surly and threatening enough.

"It's your duty as a stakeholder," I hear him say.

I take a step closer, lean against the wall, and balance the notebooks in my hand.

"Gurman, if I had anything worth telling you, I would. She's seventeen. Still a kid." Serge's voice is low and deliberate.

My stomach drops, and I press against my mouth so I don't gasp.

I'm shocked that Serge is talking to Gurman, when he's part of the very group that's tracking me. Was DeMario right?

"You forget I'm the one who had sessions with her." Gurman's voice rises. "She may be a kid, but she's sharp and cunning."

"So what do I do?" Serge's voice is suddenly despondent.

"They want the disc," Gurman says.

"I don't have anything for them."

"Give them something. Appease them."

"They'll know soon enough if it's not the right one."

"You want them killing more people? It's bad enough we've lost Corporal."

Serge says something else in muffled tones, but I can't hear him clearly.

"You're too close to her," Gurman growls.

"Close?" Serge laughs. There's an edge to his voice I've never heard before. "She's engaged to Andrew, not me."

"It's only an engagement," chides Gurman.

"Don't psychoanalyze me, Gurman. She's just a childhood friend."

"Then why is Kenders staying with you?"

"Because Paloma ran her out of her room."

"I told Tremaine you're getting a piece of ass. He understands that language."

"That's a motive he'll appreciate."

"Look. The information you now have from Hexagon ties you to them. Tremaine will never let you walk away."

A quiet moment, then . . .

"Did you hear that?" Gurman barks, and I dart down the hallway and into my bedroom. A few minutes later, Serge walks in.

"Ma chère. So, what did DeMario say?"

"She's going to have a look."

"Good." He sits down across from me. "You got nervous there today."

"I know. I know."

"What was going on? Usually you've got nerves of steel."

"Someone was following me."

"But I had your back. Why were you worried?"

I shrug, but Serge examines me as if he knows what I heard. Did he see me on his home surveillance camera? *No.* If he had, he would have changed the topic.

I look back at him. Our eyes are fixed on each other, both wondering.

Wish I could see inside that brain of yours and read your thoughts.

"Look," he says. "I'm going out on a limb for you here. I need to know I can count on you."

"Me too."

He looks at me, startled. "Ma chère?"

"Cut the French platitudes. Whose side are you on?"

37

SERGE

Stakehold

TREMAINE SPREADS his feet equidistant apart from the golf ball, his large stomach swaying as he practices his swing. "Last time we did this, I could see the dollars flashing. A new pornographic virtual world. And now . . ." He swings at the ball and whiffs it.

He gathers himself, then says, "We've got nothing."

Serge leans on his club and glares at Paloma. Only a few weeks ago, Andrew and Corporal were both standing with them. Now one is dead, and who knows if Andrew will ever return.

Tremaine casts a doubtful look at both of them. "I love playing on a real course." He turns toward the robotic caddy and grabs another club. "Do you know, I never play in Nirvana? I built a course out here instead."

Serge is well aware that Tremaine had given this same diatribe at their last golf game. At that time, Serge had looked to Corporal for a kindred spirit. This time, he keeps his head down over the ball. Serge doesn't say anything about Corporal, but he knows that everyone is dispensable in Tremaine's eyes. While he was fed the story of an accident, he would have known that wasn't the truth even if Kenders hadn't told him what she had seen. A man like Corporal doesn't have an accident.

Tremaine positions himself for another swing. "I flew over the dunes, followed the natural terrain, to find the best site. Knew a guy who knew a guy." He looks up at Serge. "Just like you. Our main stakeholder. The entrepreneur with all the connections."

He hits the ball with a knockdown swing.

"We laid down a patch of fake grass here on the best site, and created this nine-hole course." Tremaine watches the ball glide low, then turns to Serge. "We're counting on you to retrieve the information."

Paloma glares at him, her ice cold grey eyes boring into his.

"We need the disc," she says.

"More importantly," Tremaine adds, "we need the name of every person who knows."

"Knows what?" Serge plays dumb.

"The information that has been leaked."

"I'm going to plug the hole," says Paloma.

Tremaine takes two direct steps toward Serge and says, "It starts with your little piece of ass."

Serge contains the fury inside of him; corks it into his stomach till it turns and laughs with him. He can play their game.

"Find another bitch," Tremaine orders. "Get the disc from her."

"Before we lose control of the situation," Paloma pipes in.

Serge grits his teeth. "If you hadn't killed Corporal, it wouldn't have scared her away."

Paloma's face turns ashen, and her grey eyes narrow to dark lines. She says nothing.

Serge pulls the blue triangular package out of his pocket.

"I believe this is what you've been looking for."

He places it on the tee, steps into their only golf cart, and drives off.

AS SERGE drives away, Paloma watches him, and then picks up the package.

"Is that it?" she asks, and hands it to Tremaine.

He nods. "Now that we have this, we don't need her."

38

SERGE BARGES into the penthouse. "We need to leave, now." He's packing as he talks. "Paloma's tracking your digital footprint when you're in Nirvana. They're on to what Andrew is doing."

I get up from the couch slowly, and he pulls me down the hallway. "Fast, Kenders."

"My guitar. It's with Lexie."

"No time."

I struggle against the news. Ever since I confronted him about Gurman, he's been putting together a plan that he's insisting on.

"Paloma's looking for you now," Serge presses. "And the moment she finds out there's nothing on the blue holo-disc, she'll be after me, too."

"Where can we go that fast?"

"I may not control Nirvana, but I built the Bubble. I know of places they'll never find us in."

Within minutes, we're in the basement of the Bubble. We enter a room with soft monochromatic textured panels covering the walls around padded couches. I lean against the inclined wooden wall surrounding a lounge area. Serge places his palm against a pad on the wall, and a large control board hovers next to him.

He taps two fingers together, and the control board moves closer to him. He swipes one finger in a semicircular motion, and the walls fold back to reveal a dome-shaped screen that wraps three-quarters of the way around the room. The lounge shifts forward until the screen is large enough to fill my entire field of vision, and a console appears from the wall.

"What a great room," I say as I turn around in circles, taking it all in.

"A great space inspires great thinking."

We look at each other, and share a momentary smile. It's what his dad had said when we built the treehouse in his backyard. Our "maison dans les arbres." He had taken us from hardware stores to garage sales, where we picked out anything we wanted to put in our hideout. Serge's father worked tirelessly on the house until it had everything that we wanted: a rope to swing down with, a fake glass wall, a spy telescope, a trapdoor. It had been a perfect hideaway from our troubled worlds.

While Serge types away at a holographic keyboard, I look at the walls. They are upholstered in red silk, an element of our treehouse still. Back then, it was an old blanket that my mom was willing to part with, and we draped it over the one wall that was drafty. We ended up using it as our bulletin board, and hung posters and secret notes there.

Serge grabs my hand. "Come with me." We step aside, he taps a button on the control board, and the seats disappear through a trapdoor. A single folding panel slides back to reveal a large console.

"Conceal technology," Serge says. He walks to the desk and pulls out two chairs from underneath. "Welcome to my inner world, ma chère."

"Hexagon can't come in here?"

"They can't see in here, and they can't come in here. Not till we get out," he says with a wink. "I'm a step ahead of them."

A blue screen pops out of the wall, and he places his hand onto it, then takes mine and does the same thing. After a minute, the screen retreats. He walks me to the other side of the room, and presses my thumb to a pad on the wall. A door opens, and the room behind us returns back to the sitting area it was.

"There. Now you are the only other person to have access to every-thing," Serge says. "Your handprint will open any door or room in the Bubble, the bank, my safety deposit box."

We enter a large, cold room where a low whirring sound can be heard.

"We're in the Bubble's brain," Serge says. He flicks on a screen and swipes through feeds of security cameras pointing to the areas we just came through. Inside his living room, we see Paloma turning over the furniture.

"Go ahead," he prods, pushing me to a door. He explains exactly where I should go to meet him.

"Where are you going?" I ask.

"I need to create a diversion."

I don't move.

He pushes me along. "Go now. I'll see you in a bit."

I move down the hallway, and turn right. I rush to the door, but it's locked. I push against it but it doesn't budge. Serge said it would open. I turn around and run back down the hallway, but he's already left.

I head back to the door, pulling my earrings out and twisting the posts into an L and J shape. I feed them into the lock, turn them, and try the handle again.

The door opens.

I run down the long corridor, my steps echoing in the narrow cham-ber, my pulse pounding at my temples.

Another door. This time the lock won't budge, and there is no keyhole.

I look around for another door out, but I don't see one.

Did I miss a turn?

I turn back and look closely at the handle. I press my thumb into the centre, and the door swings open. *My handprint.*

I run miles down the stairs, and find myself right in front of the grey door Serge told me to wait by. A static screen appears before my eyes, and I press my thumb to it, just as Serge had done earlier. To my surprise, I can scroll through the camera feeds, just as he did.

I see Serge back in the room with the dome-shaped screen, typing away at the control board. I gasp when I see Paloma on the next screen, approaching the room, a knife in her hand.

39

A HONK outside the door draws my attention from the screen, and I peer out the peephole. It's Serge in a bright yellow mini RV.

I push on the heavy door, walk into the open air, and step into the car, perplexed. "What happened? I saw you on the screen. Paloma was running . . ."

"I'll tell you more later," he says. "It was my diversion." He plops a map in my lap. "Right now, you're the navigator."

"Don't you have GPS?"

"Yes, but we don't want them to track us. It's a good old-fashioned paper map without a digital trace."

I orient the map in my hand.

"You know how to use one of these?" Serge asks.

"Definitely. I was a girl scout."

He laughs. "You always were the one with better direction."

When we pull away, we're miles from the actual Bubble. The dome shape looms far in the distance. Serge explains that we were on the perimeter in the basement, which acts as a holding zone for all the important elements of the compound, from electronics and servers to heating and water systems. The long corridors I ran down for miles took me beyond the borders they'd ever think of searching. Apparently, the Serge I saw on the video was a holograph and he was leading Paloma in a different direction of the Bubble.

Although the basement area has limited access and we could have hidden there for a long time, we want to have the edge on them, so we keep moving. Serge has created diversions within the building that will keep them searching for us for a while before they think of looking elsewhere. His electronics within his own home are folded up and hidden behind walls. In the building itself, even on the basement level, there are rooms within rooms, set up as a safety measure against vandals. It will buy us hours of time.

"What's with the yellow colour, Serge?" I inquire.

"It reminds me of what France used to be like. Tournesol en français. Fields of sunflowers."

"Won't we stand out like a sore thumb?"

"Maybe that's the point," he says with a wink.

I lean my head against the window and watch the new scenery unfold. Unlike in the Hexagon compound, there is more life here, even if there isn't any green. Sun. Bedrock. Isn't this how life once began? I see promise in these undercurrents.

"How far behind us will she be?" I ask nervously.

"She's good with a knife, but not so swift otherwise." Serge taps his fingers against the steering wheel. "She'll only find us if we let her."

Two hours later, we turn down a side road and draw up to a small dilapidated cabin. After a quick lunch, Serge checks Paloma's whereabouts on his digital tracker. While he was leaving a digital trail for her to follow through the Bubble, he had a tracking device attached to her car.

"Robots are the most loyal and trusted staff," he says with a smirk.

He takes out a shovel and digs a hole in the loose earth, then pulls a small holo-phone from his bag and buries it just below the surface.

"This will keep them going in the wrong direction and guessing for a while." He looks up at me. "You know what to do?"

40

NIRVANA

Torrance

DUSK SETTLES on the collection of rock cairns, and I look up to catch the first bright stars dotting the sky. I lift a finger and trace out the Big Dipper, then Andrew outlines Orion's Belt. I wait for him to pull out a telescope as Andrew did when we had our first Nirvana experience at Torrance, but instead, he takes my hand in his. We trace the imaginary lines through the sky, from the North Star to the constellation of Cassiopeia. He adds one more star to the "W" of Cassiopeia to form a chair shape, and then looks ahead to locate the Great Square of Pegasus. He rests his finger on the star of the Great Square closest to Cassiopeia, the head of Andromeda, and taps firmly in the palm of my hand.

It's a spring sky, and the sister galaxy isn't visible, but unless Paloma is an astronomer, she won't know where Andromeda should be. Andrew is telling me where to go: the cave by his cottage up north near the Muskokas, where he first showed me the constellation, Andromeda.

Then he turns to me. "I don't have much time. Leave the holo-disc at the Thomas Fisher Rare Book Library. In our corner," he instructs.

"It's still standing?"

"Part of it."

The seed has been planted. Now Serge will watch their trail, and hope they follow the false clue.

Andrew takes my hand. "I have to go."

My heart drops at those four words. All I've had are these brief exchanges with him. In this Torrance experience we had saved in Nirvana, my virtual Andrew would now pull out the telescope and point out constellations.

Instead, Andrew drops his jacket onto the moss-covered rock, winks, and lowers my body onto it. Our mouths lock while our hands unbutton shirts and unzip pants, pulling clothes off of arching bodies. We make love to the rhythm of the whippoorwill's song, and then lie in each other's arms, staring at the stars.

It's not part of this experience, but there isn't any further message he has to send. This moment is only decoded by our hearts.

41

SERGE GENTLY shakes me awake. "You're dreaming, ma chère," he whispers.

I blink, and finally my lids open. I stare into the dark night, wishing that Torrance had been part of my dream, but it's always the same: the image of Corporal's bloody body. Nothing can erase it from my mind. It's a nightmare, and even when I open my eyes, it's still before them. I shift in the car seat, and try to reposition my body.

"Why don't you sleep in the back?" Serge motions to the couch.

I shake my head. "I want to stay here with you."

"Try this." Serge folds up his jacket and places it behind my head.

I claw my fingers into his skin and beg, "Stay with me."

"I'm here," Serge says softly, continuing to drive.

The moment his hand leaves my side, however, I feel a sudden panic.

"Can you hold me?" I whisper.

Serge pulls to the side of the road, and slips in behind me on the couch in the back of the RV. When his strong arms wrap around me, in my mind we are back in the treehouse days. I would run to the safe haven whenever my father entered the house, panicked until Serge was in the same room with me.

But this is different. We're not ten years old. We're running together, and the threat is much greater than my father.

Still, I drift off to sleep.

When I wake the next morning, I lift my head slightly and squint at the light.

"How did you sleep?" Serge whispers in my ear.

"Really well," I say with surprise, partly because of the uninterrupted sleep, and partly because Serge's arms are still wrapped around me. "How long was I out?"

"About six hours." His breath is warm on my check. "It's still early. Try and catch a few more hours."

I doze, but I wake up a while later, drenched from another dream. Serge isn't next to me, and I can feel the motion of the car. I look up, and see his eyes watching me through the rear-view mirror.

He pulls briefly to the side of the road. "We need to go," he says quietly, handing me a breakfast bar and plopping a small device in front of me. "We've been over this before, but you need to be clear on it."

I wave him off. "It's too complicated. I can't wrap my head around it."

He grabs on to my wrists firmly. "You have to. If we get separated . . ."

"That won't happen."

"Anything can happen out there. It's important."

Serge opens the round holo-pager, and a holographic screen pops up. "I've recoded it. I'll always know where you are, and vice versa," he explains.

"How?"

"It has my co-ordinates. It's like a built-in camera. That's the simplest way to describe it."

He swipes diagonally, and our co-ordinates pop up on the screen. He taps twice, and an image of us sitting here appears.

"Got it?" he asks.

I nod.

He steps away, and I see every movement he makes on the screen via the camera. "There, you see me waving? It's real time." His brow furrows for a moment. "If anything happens to me, you need to disable this function by pulling out the button. The moment it disengages, it's automatically destroyed."

"Then how do I find you?"

"You don't. If I'm in danger, you need to disengage, otherwise you're at risk also. They can find you. Promise me that."

I take a big gulp.

"I will."

The words are easy to say, but the notion isn't effortless to accept. I don't know where I'm going anymore, and wonder if this is all a mistake. Maybe Serge is right; someone could be playing with me in Nirvana, setting me up.

"Go over the drill with me," Serge says.

I take a deep breath, like I always do before hitting the initial chord of the first song at a gig. Settling myself.

"The moment I reach the cave, I shut off the watch. All digital off. Just wait."

"And if I'm in danger?"

Another deep breath.

"You promised, Kenders," Serge insists.

"I disengage the holo-pager."

"That's it," he says as he packs up our things, avoiding my eyes the entire time.

While Serge drives, his eyes straight ahead, I wonder how this will all pan out. It seems to me like we're driving into a desert wasteland. What could possibly be out here to protect us?

The cave might still be there, but will the cottage, or anything else, still be standing?

I look over at Serge, who's facing the road as if it's some beacon for us. I try small talk, but that doesn't work. From the way Serge grips the steering wheel, I can tell that he's tense. It could be from lack of sleep, but his downcast eyes can't hide his true feelings.

Does he think we won't make it?

"What's up, Serge?"

"Just thinking."

"Won't you talk about it?"

He shrugs.

"You're making me nervous," I admit.

"It's nothing, ma chère."

His smile is forced, but I leave it at that. What else should he be thinking at this point? He's left his Bubble behind–his creation–to follow the scant words of someone who appears for a few seconds to me in Nirvana. Wouldn't I have my doubts, too?

We arrive at a fork in the road.

"See the trail up ahead?" Serge asks.

"Uh huh."

"Follow it. There's a bend, and you'll come to an area of bedrock. That's the cave."

The cave? It doesn't look anything like it did when I came here with Andrew. But then, nothing does anymore. Lakes dried up, and forests crumpled. The whole Earth looks different.

"Wait in the cave," Serge continues.

"Why?"

"No time to explain. Just stay in that cave, and don't come out for anything."

"Where are you going?"

"I need to create a diversion."

We haven't been apart in a long time, and I've become strangely dependent on Serge. I turn the door handle and muster up my courage.

"See you soon," I say, and then I shut the door.

"Kenders, wait," he calls out. He rolls down the window, and hands me a small bag. "Keep that for me."

As I take the bag from him, he holds on to my hand, and lingers there for a moment.

"Thanks," he says.

"Sure."

I squint into the sunlight and wave as he drives off.

42

PALOMA

Scuttle

"I'VE FOUND them," Zach says as he pounds away at his holo-tablet. "Take that trail." He points toward the mountain.

The jeep swerves up the hill along a bumpy road. Two more vehicles follow.

"Are you sure?" Paloma barks, her eyes darting into the rear-view mirror.

Zach nods, although reluctantly.

"They weren't at that cabin. Now we're going in the other direction. We've been driving through nothing but desert for the last half hour. What could be out here?"

"The best place to hide," says Zach.

"If you're wrong," she says as she waves her finger, "I'll leave you out here."

Zach gulps, and keeps tracking his indicator on the screen.

They turn a corner, driving through what was once a forest, with tree trunks and branches scattered across the land. A coyote darts out in front of the jeep, and Paloma drives straight over it without even flinching.

Ahead she sees a bright yellow RV-type military vehicle on the top of the hill.

"Idiots. In plain daylight," she sneers.

"Because they never thought we'd find them," Zach affirms.

She reverses the jeep, then drives back over the coyote carcass and continues farther down the bend. She pulls up a video feed of the other two jeeps, and talks to her backup team. "I want each of you to circle around to the other sides of this hill. Someone might escape, and I don't want anyone getting away."

They nod in unison.

"I'm going in by foot. Stand by until you get my signal."

She steps out of the jeep, flings a few knives into their side holsters, and runs into the stand of bare trees.

Paloma crawls along the ground like a spider, climbing over rocks until the RV is in clear view. She scuttles along the forest floor, her palms flat on the ground, until she reaches the RV and can edge her body along the siding. She claws her fingers around the doorknob, opens it wide, and leaps up the stairs. In an instant, she flings two knives in both directions.

A sinister cackle comes from the far end of the trailer. Paloma slinks along the wall with another knife in her hand, then bounds into the room just as a bullet enters her chest. She collapses against the wall, her knife landing upright in her own leg.

A big smile crosses Serge's face. "Don't ever threaten Kenders again."

From behind her back, Paloma retrieves a smaller knife. With the last of her strength, she hurls it at Serge. It slices silently into his shoulder.

He just laughs, and fires a bullet into each of her hands. "That's for killing Kenders' cat."

Then his smile fades. He takes a deep breath, and presses a button on a box next to him.

The trailer erupts into a large fireball, shards of metal flying in the air, sparks lighting up dry tree trunks like tinder.

PALOMA'S BACKUP team, watching from the base of the hill, sprint toward the black smoke rising into the sky.

"Lost her feed," yells Zach from the car. "I can't find her."

By the time they reach the vehicle, it's incinerated. They comb through the billowing smoke, but all they find are a few smouldering, shredded metal fragments from the trailer, and some unrecognizable body parts.

"She's dead," one of them calls out.

"Ya think?" snaps Zach angrily, as he sends a robot into the debris.

43

I ARRIVE at the cave, but it's damp and dingy, and I open the round holo-pager to pass the time. A holographic screen pops up. I see Serge leaning against the yellow trailer on a hillside overlooking tree trunks and branches scattered across the land. He must be taking a break.

I look at my watch. Two p.m. I wonder how long he'll be, and I stand to stretch and warm up. When I return, the screen is down, and I open the holo-pager again.

Now Serge is sitting down inside the trailer. What kind of a diversion is this? While I'm here freezing my butt off in a cold cave, he's relaxing. He'd better get back soon. My eyes dart around the room; there's something here I'll have to tease him about.

I see a knife slam into the wall, Serge flinches, and then the screen goes blank. *Serge.* I turn off the holo-pager and turn it back on again, but his screen is still blank.

Something isn't right.

The handle of that knife blade was the same as the knife that Paloma used when she killed Corporal.

I bolt to the entrance of the cave, and in the distance I see black smoke billowing. I run back to the holo-pager but I can't see anything, just the emptiness of the screen, the thick darkness of death.

My heart starts pounding; my palms are sweating. I've never felt so helpless in my life. I have no idea where Serge is, and I could never get to him in time. There's got to be something I can do, but I can't think of anything.

I talk myself through it. I'm sure this is a delayed feed. The smoke is the diversion Serge talked about. He'll be back here in no time.

But half an hour later, I'm still waiting.

You need to disengage, otherwise you're at risk also. They can find you. Promise me that.

What if Serge was captured? I need to help him.

But he had asked me. His one promise.

Disengage. Promise me that.

I press the button, and disconnect the feed.

I disengage the holo-pager. Shut off the watch.

The smoke still twists into the sky.

I wait. They'll be looking for me next.

THE SUN scorches the valley, but I stand outside and watch the smoke rising. I can't stay in the dimly-lit cave; the darkness scares me. Yes, I'm frightened.

Even in the warm sun, I'm still shaking. I saw Corporal killed in front of my eyes, and I won't accept that it has now happened to Serge.

Serge had said it was a diversion. I assure myself it was a delayed feed. But what if something went wrong?

I play through the entire day in my mind. Serge had been on edge after I woke up, but he wouldn't have planned this situation. He would have said good-bye to me, at least.

Or would he?

My pulse quickens at the thought of Paloma hunting him down. These thoughts stop my shaking and turn to anger, and I heat up.

I won't return to the darkness of that cave. It's a reminder of my world closing in. I move into the crook of a rock where there's an ounce of shade left.

And a snake.

I step back. I can't risk another move and chance it striking. My eyes shift downward, to the curled serpent by my feet. I don't move a muscle, and just lean my head into the cool shadow of the rock.

I'm trapped, unless the snake is as scared as I am.

Are they the only creatures left on Earth? Or the only ones that venture out in this heat? Where is everything else? All the dangers they talk of at Hexagon. The feral animals. The survivors.

I look down at my watch. How I'd love to escape into Nirvana one more time, to talk with Andrew before I melt into parchment out here.

I try to slow down my breathing. I can't stay here forever, but Serge said to wait.

He *will* show up.

But . . . what do I do if he doesn't?

The sun blinds my eyes, and I close them, terrified. I've always been afraid of snakes, but this is my first close encounter with one, and it's worse than I imagined. If this desolate blank landscape is all that remains, without Serge, without Andrew . . . if it's just me and this stark dune of an Earth, the snake might as well do me a favour and bite me.

Kill me before Paloma does.

I hear a sound close by, and I press my body flat against the rock, not wanting to threaten the snake in any way.

What if this was a plot all along? Just like Gurman told Serge in his office. The information has been distributed, but I know too much. The details, the string of people, the chains of command . . . the entire story rests with me.

A gunshot rings out, and the snake snaps its tail into the air and uncoils.

I reach for a loose rock, my heart pounding, and then I hear Andrew's voice.

"That's venomous," he says, kicking the dead snake.

I blink. Then blink again. It's him.

Am I hallucinating?

I just stare at him, blank faced. I want to say something, but I can hardly think.

"Let's go where it's safe," he says. He hands me a canteen of water, and I can barely lift it to my mouth.

He wraps his hand around mine, supporting it, holding the bottle up to my lips, wiping the water that drips down my chin.

He cups his hands around my face, and our foreheads touch. We breathe each other in, separating this moment from the last two weeks, wrapping our arms around each other to lock it in. His lips find mine, softly at first, and then with a hard longing.

"It's you," I keep saying whenever I come up for air.

"I'm here," Andrew reassures me. "I'm here."

My hands start shaking, and I never want to let him go. *Never.*

44

SAFETY IS deep in the bowels of a remote outpost that used to be a research station, and is now a weathered facility buried deep in Canadian Shield bedrock. It's a stark, foreboding place, but with Andrew at my side, it feels like home.

We travelled here, barrelling through the hills and valleys on an ATV. I sat on the back, holding on to Andrew's body.

Still holding.

The entrance is hidden in a series of rock channels and caves that we squeeze through. When we lock the first door and park the vehicle, Andrew says, "Now you're safe."

"Is this where you were the whole time?" I ask.

He nods.

"How did you get here?"

"I escaped from Hexagon. I didn't want to leave you that way, but I had no choice. Tremaine came to my office with an ultimatum. We had a steaming argument. He wanted me to stop my research and focus on pornography. I told him the metrics weren't set for that. He said he controlled the direction of research, and that all my work was owned by the company. That I would be terminated on the spot if I wouldn't deliver what he asked for. I called his bluff–but, this time it wasn't one.

"So I had to act fast. I argued a bit, while all the time I was downloading everything to the holo-disc hidden inside the picture frame at the lab. Then I erased everything from the computer. At the time he didn't know I was doing it, but there would be nothing in the system later when he checked.

"When I left, I couldn't head home. I had to run far away, because they'd be after me. And I couldn't clear my desk or take anything, not even the picture frame. They marched me straight to my car."

For the first time, I realize what Andrew must have gone through. The fear he was under, for himself, and then for me.

"Why didn't you call me?" I demand.

"It was too risky."

"I thought you were dead."

"I know."

"And those moments in Nirvana . . . I wasn't sure if it was really you or my imagination or my longing. Or Hexagon. Serge thought it was . . ." My breath stops for a second, and guilt washes over me. I was so taken by seeing Andrew again, that I forgot about Serge.

"Did you hear from Serge?" I ask.

"Not yet."

"I want to go back for him."

I head for the door, but Andrew grabs me. "It's too dangerous," he protests.

"All the more reason Serge shouldn't be out there."

I try to break free of Andrew's arms, but he holds me tightly.

"He risked his life for me. I won't leave him. I won't," I insist.

"Kenders, if he's alive, he'll contact us. We'll go get him. I promise. When we can. When it's safe."

"Who's 'we'? How did Serge get involved in this? What's going on?" My mind is twisting up inside.

"Kenders, sit tight. I'll tell you everything once we're in the Hive."

"The Hive?"

A smile crosses his face, and he grabs my hand.

I follow him like a puppy. We crawl down a series of steel staircases that lead to a long concrete tunnel. At the end of it, we find a metal door. I'm waiting for a card swipe or an electronic keypad, but Andrew pulls out a metal key.

"This is an old facility, back from the nineteen eighties," he explains.

"How did you find it?"

"We've got a few of these," Andrew says, his muscles flexing as he yanks the heavy door open. "Hexagon funded us, but that doesn't mean we put all their money into their research initiatives. We funnelled enough of it into building our own labs underground to continue the work they didn't want us to complete."

We pass through two more security areas before Andrew opens a final door and says, "Welcome to the Hive."

Everyone looks up when we step inside. A murmur settles over the large room as people stop their work, point, and get up from their chairs. It's the size of an auditorium, with glassed-in labs running along the entire length of each side, which lead to a long grey corridor.

Terk stops talking to a team of programmers in the back corner and runs over to us. He holds me at arm's length.

"When did you get out?" I ask.

"Before the Red Door got reinstated."

"I never thought I'd see you again."

He ruffles my hair. "I knew you'd make it."

I'm speechless at first. Did he know about the Hive too?

"You knew?"

Terk smiles. "All along."

Now I wonder how Terk got here. Who everyone is.

As if reading my mind, Andrew says, "Anyone we could save from the Red Door is here."

"How did you get them out?"

"When I recoded them, I changed their Hexagon identities. They left on a food supply transport to the Bubble, and then we got them out of there."

"How?" I press.

"There are people working on the inside at the Bubble, within Hexagon, to help the Hive and bring Tremaine down," says Terk.

"Even I don't know all of it," says Andrew. "I spent my time working on Nirvana, and digging deeper into Hexagon's system."

"What about Corporal?"

"He was a key part of this," Andrew says in a sullen tone.

Andrew reaches for my left hand and squeezes it, but I don't reciprocate. I feel like I've been slapped. The Hive was here all along. It seems that everyone close to me knew about it.

Terk introduces me to his band of technologists, but I barely retain the names. Apparently everyone wants to meet me, but it's all a blur.

Andrew makes excuses for me, explaining that I'm tired and have been through a lot. He leads me into his office down the hallway. It's very different from the high tech lab he had worked in before our lives blew up.

He points to the tattered wooden desk. "This is where I was when I communicated with you in Nirvana."

I look at the bare walls, the push pins in cork boards, the large mainframe computer, the pens and paper. Each time I saw his face, however briefly, I imagined him in the world we knew, not an antiquated time from one hundred years ago. During these last two weeks, this is where he was calling out to me from.

I sit down, clutching on to my backpack and Serge's bag, my entire life condensed to these two items in my hands.

"It's all too much, isn't it?" Andrew asks gently.

I shrug. "I feel like everyone knew about this place but me."

His soft brown eyes open wide. "It's not like that. I was going to tell you. Remember? But then it all blew up when Tremaine came in."

I remember that night. The "tell you over coffee" code.

"I couldn't have done this without you," he continues. "You're the one who retrieved the holo-discs. There was no one else I'd have given them to. Not Terk. Not Corporal. Only you."

He gestures back to the room.

"Everything here. Everything we've worked on depends on the holo-discs you retrieved. Everyone here knows that. Without you, we'd be starting over."

I consider this information, but still. "Why didn't you trust me before? Others knew."

He lifts my left hand to his lips. "I was protecting you. Everyone involved was risking their life every day. I couldn't let anything happen to you." He rubs the back of his thumb over my knuckles. "When I first reached out to you in Nirvana, it was just to let you know I was alive. I was hoping you'd read between the lines."

I choke back my emotion, and take a deep breath.

"I thought you were dead at first. I wasn't sure about anything. And then when they took me to the morgue . . ." I bury my face in my hands and just shake my head. I can't ever think of that day. "It was when you winked at me and used our code: 'You can tell me over coffee.' Then I knew it wasn't a loop. That you were really behind the virtual you."

He's already nodding at me. "I couldn't stay long, though, or Hexagon could trace it. It killed me not to talk to you, console you, make sure you were all right. But I had to get that information into your hands. The decoy disc from the lab is what kept you alive, since they knew you had something they wanted."

"Until they got it."

"That's where Serge came in." Andrew grits his teeth. "It was a risk, because I didn't trust him." He looks away, and then back at me. "You know that."

I nod. There was always a tension between them, ever since Andrew and I started dating. They were both cordial in my presence, but I knew they were being civil out of love for me. If it were up to Andrew, Serge would be out of my life, and vice versa.

DeMario walks into the room and straight up to Andrew and I.

I gasp.

"Yes," Andrew says. "She's the one who indoctrinated me here."

DeMario smiles at both of us. "Glad you're both safe," she says, then she opens a holo-file and gets down to business. "Andrew, have you seen this?"

He swipes through a few digital files and chuckles. He puts his hand on my shoulder, and leads DeMario and I back into the central room. When Andrew enters with the two of us, the room grows quiet.

Andrew pulls out the discs I retrieved, holding them up for everyone to see. "We have the proof that Hexagon deliberately killed off the bee population, and has suppressed emerging technologies that could bring them back." DeMario hands him the memory stick. "And a copy of Oblick's research, so he can continue," he adds.

Everyone hoots and whistles, and bodies emerge from various rooms to join in the celebration.

At the back of the room, the crowd separates, and a grey-haired man walks toward us. He puts his arm around Andrew in a long embrace, and then turns to me.

"I'm Oblick," he introduces himself.

"Oblick already has a hive of experimental bees near this facility," Andrew explains.

"We've digitally masked them from satellite detection," Terk adds, "and have located them out in the wild."

Oblick reaches for the memory stick from Andrew, and looks at it over the brim of his glasses. He turns it over in his hands and stares at it for a long time, as if waiting for an answer.

What is he thinking? Can he really do this?

A group is forming around the old man and me. Andrew and Terk take a step back.

"I had developed a theory," Oblick says. "Hexagon offered to buy me out for a hundred million."

One hundred million dollars?

"I refused." He looks around the room. "We know what happened then. They funded my research, wanting to direct it."

He looks back at me, bemused. "I refused."

I know where this story is going. They discredited him, and he wasn't heard of again. DeMario told me in the church.

Oblick removes his glasses, and looks directly into my eyes. "And then you came along."

I don't get it. I look to him for explanation.

"Some of those suppressed files on that memory stick are mine."

So that's what's in there. *No wonder everyone wanted it.*

He hands it back to Andrew, and then holds out both hands to me. "My research . . . you've returned it to me."

Andrew sees me wince as I shake Oblick's hand. He pulls me aside as everyone begins to crowd around Oblick to talk about the next steps.

Andrew gently takes my hand from behind my back and opens it. The palm is purple and swollen.

"It's nothing," I say. "Just a bruise."

"We've got a full medical facility here. I'm going to have them look at that right now."

"Have you heard from Serge yet?" I ask.

"Your hand first," Andrew says as he leads me down the hall.

45

MY HAND is fine, but the rest of my body has hit an exhaustion point. I get a strong sedative and have a long sleep. I wake up in the medical room, and look around me. It's well equipped with machines that you'd see in any hospital ER. How much money did they siphon off of Hexagon's funding, anyway?

I look in the mirror. If you compared this face to the Madison poster, you'd probably walk right by me. And yet, I'm the same person.

If the Hive is now my underground life, what will become of who I was? My music? Chopper?

I had the option to stay in the Bubble with Serge and live a comfortable life, as Lexie was doing. But I couldn't do that without Andrew.

Serge.

I haven't seen him yet, and a shiver runs through me.

I pull a blanket around my shoulders, and step barefoot into the hallway. Just then, Andrew turns the corner.

"How are you feeling?" he asks.

"Better," I say.

He takes my bandaged hand gently in his. "It's going to be swollen."

"I won't be strumming for a while."

I stand and look at him. I can still barely believe that he's here in front of me. It's a lot to take in.

"Where's Serge?" I ask.

Andrew places his hand on the small of my back, and leads me into a boardroom. "That's a long story."

"Did he know all along?"

"He knew, but he hadn't made a choice one way or another. He was conflicted for a long time."

"What made him decide?"

"You."

My heart sinks. He did all of this for me?

Andrew swipes open a large holo-screen. "I just saw this now. You need to watch it alone," he says.

"Why?"

"You know I love you."

I nod, not sure where this is going.

"So does Serge."

Andrew dims the lights and leaves.

ON THE screen Serge appears, sitting on his balcony in the Bubble.

"Ma chère. If you're watching this, then you're safe, and for that I'm so grateful."

He looks out at the ocean scene, then back to the camera.

"You know why I chose this backdrop? It was our loveliest time together. Here at the Bubble. I hoped that it could be more, but life got in the way. I've been working with Andrew to help retrieve his research and keep it secure. I even helped get you out of that research building. I knew it was rigged to blow once you were in it, so I arranged a thirty second digital feed delay to facilitate your escape."

He looks down for a few moments, and then back up. "I did it to keep you safe, but it didn't end there. I had to get that pit bull Paloma off your tail, and there was only one way to do it. Someone had to maintain a digital signal Paloma could follow, in the belief that it was you. But I was the one waiting for her."

My stomach plummets. Serge was in the trailer. A diversion, he had said. *You were going to be right back.*

"I had to get rid of Paloma forever for you, and to stop Hexagon looking for you. The only way to do that was to make sure they'd find two bodies inside, and that happened. One belongs to Paloma. The other belongs to a man they will believe to be Andrew, thanks to dental bridges and DNA evidence that I coerced Andrew into providing. Andrew had no idea why I was asking for this, but I always had a backup plan for the two of you in case things went wrong, which they often do."

He looks long and hard at the camera, and takes a deep breath.

"That second body in the trailer . . . is me."

I gasp. No! *No no no.*

"Remember our treehouse, ma chère? We always called it our haven. All those years ago, in the dusky light of our treehouse, there was a blurred line for me between building our safe little world and playing house with you. And that's what I felt when we sat on the balcony here a few weeks ago, if just for a moment. I let my imagination fill in what was missing in our lives. Even when we were kids, we gave each other support as friends, but I always sensed something more. Well, maybe I hoped for it. And when I look at you now, the beautiful, talented woman, your soft flowing hair, the youthful curve of your shoulders, your . . ."

Serge has a distant look in his eyes, and I feel what he wants to say.

He corrects himself, in the only way he can, with a chuckle. "You're a far cry from the scrawny girl you were back then. But even then, you were beautiful. Even then, Kenders, I loved you."

Serge. I felt the same way, too. I did. And maybe if Andrew hadn't come along, we'd be together, you and I . . . but it didn't happen. And now you're dead. So many people dead. Corporal, too. All for me . . . all for Andrew.

I can see that Serge is gathering himself, trying to stay bright when inside his heart must be breaking. All the dreams he had. Hopes of us together. Did I even know?

Of course I did.

Why didn't I ever say something? How do you approach a topic like that with your closest friend? I just hoped it would go away. What a gift he has given me. He has given the world.

"I don't want to say goodbye like this, but if I had told you, I know you never would have walked away from the car. You'd have needed to save me, like you do every little creature on the planet. It wouldn't have worked."

My chest locks, and I can't breathe.

"I've been in love with you since we were kids, ma chère. I had to settle for being in your life as a friend, but it was still an honour. And now, because I'm so in love with you, I leave you in the same way."

He reaches for something on the table, and pulls out a holo-disc. "I gave you a bag. It has every song of yours, way back to the treehouse days. I want you to have them." He smiles gently. "I guess you could say, I was your biggest fan."

Serge presses his fingers into the corners of his eyes, composing himself.

"And there are a few other things. It's all in there."

My vision is blurred by a stream of tears. This can't be.

It can't be.

"Why a backup plan for the two of you?"

I lift my hands to my face, wiping the tears away.

"Because I know you love Andrew. I know you couldn't be happy without him."

I love you, too. You're my oldest friend. I need you, Serge. I need you.

He places his hands together as if in prayer. "So, the future of the world is now in your hands. You have the research you need to bring back the bees, and the proof you need to bring Hexagon down. The people necessary to help are in place. But it won't be easy. They know you are out there, and they're using everything in their power to find you."

He looks at me. Yes, me. Right through the screen, as if he is here in the room with me, his eyes soft, maybe even wet.

"Be safe, ma chère. I love you."

The screen goes blank.

"Wait!" I put my hand to the empty screen. "I love you," I say. "I always loved you."

I lean my forehead against the screen as tears drop onto the floor. I don't want to see anyone. Not even Andrew.

46

HOURS LATER, I'm still sitting in the dark room. I replay the video one more time, pausing on Serge's face, waiting for him to come back to life on his own.

It's Andrew who finally walks in.

He pulls me toward him, and my body follows. I sink into the softness of his touch, the familiar warmth of his body. For a moment, I rest my head against his shoulder. I find comfort there, until the sorrow settles back over me like a wave.

"Could he still be alive? The video could be a delayed feed," I whisper.

"Not possible."

"He did it at your lab when I retrieved the holo-disc. He *was* alive. He did it to save me then."

"This is different."

"He risked his life." I jab my finger into the air to cork my sadness. "I don't want to leave a stone unturned."

"If we go out there, Kenders, we risk this entire operation." Andrew hesitates for a moment. "And your life. The one thing Serge wanted to protect more than his own safety."

I bite my lip to quell the tears; hold back the flood gates.

"It wasn't supposed to go like this." Andrew hangs his head. "We were all supposed to end up here together."

He reaches for my hand, but it rests limply in his.

"When did Serge know he'd die?" I ask. I think back to our last night together. And that quiet drive toward the cave.

"He didn't. We had a few plans, but blowing up the trailer was his last resort. And his idea."

I want to burst into tears but I force them down, swallow them into the depths of my body. I've lost Corporal, the man who was the closest thing to a real father that I might ever get. Then Serge, the one who was like my brother.

All I have left is Andrew.

And a world we have to rebuild. *The future of the world is now in your hands,* Serge told me at the end of his video.

I don't even know where to start. I'm a reactive kind of person; Andrew is the planner.

The weeks catch up with me. Everything that's happened, everyone I've lost. I'm mentally and emotionally spent, and I take Andrew's hands in mine. This is our first day back together. I can't let anything impede on that.

"I know how much you loved Serge," Andrew says.

"He was like a brother to me."

"I can't begin to imagine how you must feel, but I know how scared I was when I knew you were in danger. The thought of losing you . . . I'd give up if it happened."

"You can't ever do that."

"Not while I have you."

"We're starting over, but together." I feel the sadness creeping up my throat, but I push it back down. "Serge did this for me. For you. So we have a future. We have to work hard toward that."

"We will. I've been thinking about how grateful I am to him. Not only for helping get the holo-discs to us, but also for protecting you. I want to thank him in some way."

Holding back the tears just moves the sorrow to another part of my body. My lips tremble. I know this is coming from Andrew's heart. While it's a gesture of love toward me to recognize what Serge meant in my life, he truly is thankful.

My heart is so full of emotion that I feel I will explode. Mourning for Serge. Love for Andrew. Hope for the future.

I let out a deep breath. "I'd like to hold a memorial for him." I think of the funeral Hexagon held for Corporal, cold and staid and built on a lie. I want more for Serge.

"I know just the place," Andrew says.

47

ANDREW TAKES me through a woodland trail. A different forest than those we see around Hexagon and the Bubble. There's green.

"These are non-pollinating trees and plants," says Andrew. "But there's more."

He opens my palm, and lays a cloth in my outstretched hand.

"What's this?"

"You'll see." Andrew can't hold back any longer. He grabs my hand, and we run.

In the clearing, Oblick and a few other people swarm around an apple tree with paintbrushes.

"What are they doing?" I ask, fascinated.

"Pollinating trees by hand."

We stroll up to Oblick, who shows me the pollen-laden bristles on his brush.

"We're the worker bees," he says with a wink.

He explains that he stored many seeds in a vault, and now he's working with those seeds to change growth cycles and patterns. Oblick leads us to a sunflower, and he rubs from the edges to the centre of the capitulum. When he turns his palm over, it's laden with yellow powder.

"You can do the same with your cloth," he tells me.

I look around the little oasis. One woman is harvesting pollen and collecting it in a tube, while another coats her brush with the pollen and inserts it into flower petals. They're doing the job that minimal bees can't manage right now.

"We haven't named the field yet," says Andrew. "I thought it could be named for Serge."

"Tournesol," I say.

"I like it."

"It's French, for sunflowers." Serge loved the sunflower fields in France.

Andrew turns to Oblick. "Will you be planting any seeds soon?"

"Tomorrow," he says.

"We'd like to hold a memorial for Serge out here."

"I can't think of a better place. We're changing the Earth and bringing it back. The bees, these plants. He was integral to that."

"Can you really bring back the bees?" I ask Oblick.

"DeMario thinks so. She's been working on it since she got the formulas from you."

Suddenly, I gasp as I see everyone pointing to the sky. Small dots above the tree line move like a wave against the blue expanse, and then descend.

Andrew points to their hive.

Bees on Earth. They're real.

48

OBLICK STANDS in the centre of a plot of overturned earth. I can't help but think how much it looks like a freshly laid burial plot in a cemetery, but this is more poignant given our situation, and what Serge sacrificed his life for.

Oblick stands at the front of the crowd, looking like a bearded prophet with his coat tousling in the wind.

"These seeds we're laying in the gentle Earth are our life support, and we dedicate this plot of land to the memory of Serge. When there is death there is always new life, and today, we will all plant seeds in his honour."

Oblick leans on his thighs as he bends over to drop the seeds into the ground.

"Now the work is left to us, the living, to carry out Serge's vision for our future. When we are scared, we have to remember his courage. When we have doubt, we have to remember his sacrifice. Life gives and life takes away. We have to continue to give as Serge did."

Oblick nods toward Andrew, who gives my hand a squeeze and then steps forward.

Andrew clears his throat. "I was in research, and Serge was corporate. We couldn't have been more worlds apart. But we had one thing in common: a devotion to a special person."

I look at Andrew, my eyes welling with tears.

"Serge," Andrew continues, "you protected Kenders, brought her safely back. You risked your life for her, and for the cause we're fighting for. I am eternally grateful. We all are."

He gulps as he continues, the words finding themselves after a few deep breaths. "Life is a mystery. We wanted to be here together with you, Serge, building our new future. Now, because of you, we're holding on. We have much work to do to ensure that your sacrifice wasn't in vain, but we're taking this moment to grieve, because that is love." Andrew looks toward me. "And love is cherishing the person you were; being grateful for the life you blessed us with."

Andrew steps forward and scatters a series of seeds into the earth. "We will move forward because of you. We will have hope because of you. And we will love because of you."

He holds out his hand to me. I let out a deep breath, and take a step forward. I look at the people around me, all strangers a few days ago, who are now becoming familiar faces. I have lost my home, and found another one. I have lost Serge, and found Andrew.

My life as I knew it is spinning around in my head, and then I look toward the sunflowers. I gather my thoughts, and finally speak:

"Tournesol. Sunflowers, particularly in France, were a favourite sight for Serge. We're dedicating this space to you, Serge, but your spirit and memories will live on in us, as the trail you created will resonate and flow into our future."

I unfold my fingers to reveal the delicate seeds in my palm. I take each seed, one by one, place it in the earth, and then cover it. Each time I lay a seed down, I speak a silent memory to Serge. I'm aware of the many times he came to my rescue during my life. My father. Intel on lab raids. Support at concerts. And two days ago.

I place down the last seed and cover it with both of my hands, holding on to the earth, crushing it between my fingers to force back the tears.

I stand up slowly, my legs suddenly feeling weak with sorrow, my heart thumping loudly. "This very special ground here . . ." I blink back the tears, my temples pounding. " . . .will be the start of new life . . ." I sniffle and then come the tears, slipping down my cheeks.

Andrew walks up beside me and picks up where I left off. "You are more than this place, Serge. You are Spirit forever within me. And your sacrifice for my life will never be forgotten."

I'm weeping now, and Andrew puts his arm around me as he continues to read my thoughts. "You are no longer bound by this Earth, but a part of it. No longer tied to a particular place or time. You're free. Every time I smell a flower. Every time I see a tree waving in the breeze. No matter where you are, no matter how far I go in this big, wide open world, we will always be together."

Andrew asks for a minute of silence. It was planned this way, but I need it to gather myself together. I close my eyes and take a deep breath, waiting till I feel a calm enter my being. And then, without Lexie's stirring drumbeat, with my own heart as a metronome, I begin an a cappella version of "Honey," altering the lyrics at the end for Serge.

"Serge, we still feel you,

The flowers, they thank you . . ."

Andrew swipes the lyrics onto a holographic screen that rises for everyone to read. When I break down, they continue the song:

"Serge, we still feel you,

The spring buds, they thank you . . ."

Of all the times I have sung this song, this moment is the most powerful yet; more significant than my Nirvana experience at Madison. A chorus of voices for Serge. And then I sing out, with my strongest and loudest voice, the song I wrote for him:

"I don't grieve, I know you're free,

It's just a sudden loss for me.

You have been my oldest friend,

Confidant till the very end.
Know that every single day,
My thoughts will travel your way.
I love you with all my heart,
Our spirits will never be apart."

49

THREE MONTHS later, the temperature drops sharply, and group efforts turn to research inside our underground shelter. Andrew and I are in our bedroom, where he's cast the night sky on our ceiling from a video feed. It's as close to the romantic evenings we used to have at the cottage as we can get now.

I can't believe how my life has taken such a drastic turn, and how inspiring it is. For the first time, I'm not fighting something, but working toward a bright and hopeful future.

Andrew rests his feet against the wall, lifts a finger, and traces out the constellations from the North Star in the Big Dipper to Cassiopeia. He takes my hand in his, outlines the shapes that lead to the head of Andromeda, and taps firmly in my palm.

I turn toward him and laugh. "We're not in Nirvana."

"Thought you'd ask me to prove it," he says, lowering his lips onto mine.

I raise myself up on my elbows, teasing him back. "Speaking of proving, did you know about the mango?"

He smiles, and gets up to shut down the video feed as I curl up in bed and yawn. "Corporal did it. He wanted you to have hope."

Andrew opens his computer and checks something.

"You going to work for a bit?"

He nods, and comes over to kiss me goodnight.

"Did you leave the stick?" I ask.

"What stick?"

I tell him, and the blood drains from his face. He says nothing, his furrowed brows closing in on his expression.

"Get some sleep," he says.

He walks slowly from the bed, and steps from the dark room into the light of the hallway.

THE NEXT morning, I wake up late and to an empty bed. I slowly get myself ready, and then amble toward the cafeteria. I notice Terk in the hallway.

"Have you seen Andrew?" I ask him.

He shakes his head.

I go to Andrew's office. The door is open, but he's not there. I look for his backpack, but I can't find it.

I walk through the entire complex, and no one has seen Andrew. Not DeMario. Not Oblick. Not any of the crew. They start a search for him, but nothing comes up.

I start to panic. This is just like the last time, when Andrew disappeared without a trace.

I strap on my watch and enter Nirvana to search for him. I go to all of the places where he reached out to me before—the apple orchard, Madison, Torrance, Massey College—but he doesn't show up at any of them. After hours, I leave virtual reality behind, take off my watch, and start pacing the room.

There's a knock on my door, and I jump for the handle. It's Terk.

"Found him?" I ask hopefully.

"No. We can't even find his digital trace."

I sink into the wall. This can't be happening.

"Everyone has combed the area looking for him," Terk assures me.

Suddenly, I speculate that it's someone on the inside. Terk? DeMario? Even Oblick. I trust no one. Isn't that what Andrew told me?

I never asked him why he said those things. I didn't ask him so many questions I should have. And now, I'm on my own again.

I look back at Terk's eyes, searching for an answer.

"What do we do next?"

He looks down at the floor, then back up at me, and shrugs.

"Is there something you're not telling me?" I shake his shoulders, demanding an answer.

He lowers his eyes even farther. An eerie chill goes through me.

I have to look for Andrew alone.

ABOUT
J.R. STEWART

J.R. STEWART has worked on many corporate projects throughout a prolific IT academic and consulting career, and has been involved with many confidential virtual reality projects. After working on advanced "VR" technologies for over a decade, Stewart grew concerned about the implications of this work and the possible psychological effects that it may have on its users. In 2010, Stewart considered publishing a revealing account of the advances being made regarding this technology, but was concerned about the implications that a tell-all book may have on career prospects. The next year, writing under a protective pseudonym, Stewart began work on the speculative "Nirvana" series instead. Finally ready for publication, these novels present a story that is closer to reality than you may assume.

BOOK CLUB DISCUSSION QUESTIONS

1. If you could travel to Nirvana, where would you go and what would you do?

2. Do you think that virtual reality technology is good for society? Why or why not?

3. Who do you think would have been a better match for Kenders: Andrew or Serge? Why?

4. If you were Kenders, what steps would you take to find Andrew? Who would you trust?

5. Terk is a complex character. Do you think he is working with or against Kenders?

6. If you could meet one character from *Nirvana*, who would it be? What would you ask them?

7. Do you think that Andrew is alive? Why or why not?

WRITE FOR US

WE LOVE discovering new voices and welcome submissions. Please read the following carefully before preparing your work for submission to us. Our publishing house does accept unsolicited manuscripts but we want to receive a proposal first and if interested we will solicit the manuscript.

We are looking for solid writing—present an idea with originality and we will be very interested in reading your work.

As you can appreciate, we give each proposal careful consideration so it can take up to six weeks for us to respond, depending on the amount of proposals we have received. If it takes longer to hear back, your proposal could still be under consideration and may simply have been given to a second editor for their opinion. We can't publish all books sent to us but each book is given consideration based on its individual merits along with a set of criteria we use when considering proposals for publication.

THE MOST IMPORTANT THING

THE AUTHOR greatly appreciates you taking the time to read this work. Please consider leaving a review on Amazon and Goodreads, and telling your friends or blog readers about the "Nirvana" series, to help spread the word. Thank you for your support.

THANK YOU FOR READING NIRVANA

www.ingramcontent.com/pod-product-compliance
Lightning Source LLC
Chambersburg PA
CBHW072354020726
47506CB00004B/1115